Raising Hell in the Highlands

A Timeless Love Series, Book 2

(Originally published as Lost in Time II)

Abbie Zanders

This is a work of fiction. Similarities to real people, places, or events are entirely coincidental.

Raising Hell in the Highlands

(A Timeless Love Series, Book 2)

First edition (Lost in Time II). September, 2014.

Second edition (Raising Hell in the Highlands). January, 2016

Copyright © 2014-2018 Abbie Zanders.

Written by Abbie Zanders.

All rights reserved.

ISBN: 1523308931
ISBN-13: 978-1523308934

Acknowledgements

Special thanks to:

… Carol Tietsworth for her mad proofreading skills; if you find an error, I made it *after* she looked at it.

… Cindy, Susie, and Aubrey for their infinite patience and willingness to put up with me.

… Heather Black | Studio 410 Designs, for her beautiful, one-of-a-kind custom photos and cover design. (background image from pixabay.com)

… and to all of *you* for selecting this book – you didn't have to, but you did. Thanks ☺

Before You Begin

Please note that due to strong language and some steamy romantic interludes, this book is intended for mature (18+) readers. If this is not you, then

1. Shame on you.
2. Give this book to your mother (or other mature adult) and let *them* enjoy it.

Prologue

Aislinn Isobeille McKenna was a survivor.

When the brutal car crash took the life of her family - including her mother - a full month before Aislinn was even supposed to draw her first breath, she pulled through – tiny, wrinkled and screaming, but alive.

She was lucky, they'd said, to have been spared.

When the much bigger kids in the low-income housing parks where she grew up bullied her, she became quite a scrapper. She learned how to turn the most mundane items into weapons – rocks, sticks, rusty pieces of tailpipe ripped from rotting junkers – and fought back. More often than not she wound up bloodied and slightly the worse for wear, but stronger and a little smarter, too.

She was lucky, they'd said, that she was quick and resourceful enough to hold her own.

And when she entered her last tour of duty overseas with the elite Rangers – though she herself could not officially be called one at the time because of her double-X chromosomes - and her assault vehicle was blown off the road by a land mine, the medics somehow managed to piece enough of her back together to send her home, though no one else in the convoy had been so lucky.

Lucky, they'd said.

Luck had nothing to do with it.

Chapter 1

"You are lucky you get that check from the government every month," the landlord said, greedily snatching up the cash she held out to him. His fingers brushed against hers in the process, sending shudders of revulsion up and down her spine. In Aislinn's opinion, the man was one step up on the evolutionary scale from a dung beetle.

Beady black eyes leered at her, blatantly looking her up and down. The pungent aroma of his rank body odor mixed with his rancid breath; it was only through years of training and discipline that she managed to control her gag reflex. There was odious, and then there was Manny.

"*Some* people actually have to work for a living," he sneered.

Aislinn didn't rise to the bait. Manny had probably never done an honest day's work in his life. Slum-lord, drug dealer, and part-time pimp didn't count. The man was literally a boil on the ass of society.

Or at least he *was*. By tomorrow, it was doubtful Manny would be *anything*. Assuming, of course, Manny did what he always did – that is, skim a little off the top for himself before handing over the rent money to the *real* owners. They were a group of highly-motivated individuals who preferred not to be ripped-off, and were less than pleased when they received *anonymous* tips concerning Manny's entrepreneurial endeavors to create a little side-business of his own.

Yep, tomorrow was Christmas, and the hard-working, blue-collar tenants of this building would be receiving a gift in the form of one less vile rat-bastard to make their lives miserable. It wasn't much, perhaps, but it was the best she could give them under the circumstances.

"Yeah. Everyone should be so lucky," Aislinn responded in a voice devoid of emotion. She forced the door closed in his unshaven face and exhaled heavily.

If he only knew what she had done to receive that monthly check. What she had seen. War. Blood. Carnage. Death. All of her life people had been telling her she was lucky, but she sure as hell didn't feel that way.

So she had a knack for not dying when everyone else around her did. Could that really be considered luck? How was it a good thing to be the only one left behind, to have people look at her, wondering *why*? What made her so fucking special?

Maybe the ones who *didn't* make it were the lucky ones. Freed from living in a world of violence and hate, they were beyond the pettiness and greed that polluted the land and the air and the hearts of so many. Whether you believed in some utopian form of afterlife or not, whatever came next had to be better.

Unless, of course, you were riding the express lane straight to Hell.

Aislinn didn't think she was, but what did she know? Maybe the road to Hell really was paved with good intentions, in which case there was already a special pool of fire and brimstone with her name on it.

These dismal thoughts and a thousand disheartening memories drifted through her mind. She surfed over them on the half-bottle of Jack Daniels, looking down impassively as if she was watching someone else's life instead of her own.

Had it been a movie, it would have done lousy at the box office. One unfortunate occurrence after another, without the occasional comic relief or romantic interest to make it bearable. Scenes of death, of malice, of poverty and cruelty flowing seamlessly from one minute to the next. By the halfway point, most people would have left their seats in search of something better. Those who managed to grit their teeth and last a bit longer would have no doubt been those rare, optimistic souls who always held out hope for a happy ending, though there seemed little chance of that at this point.

Was this the end, she wondered? Or would there be another day, and another, a seemingly endless series of days that stretched out farther and farther, until there just wasn't anything left?

She was so tired. So very tired. At barely twenty-five years old, Aislinn McKenna could feel things were drawing to a close.

The sad little solitary string of Christmas lights – an impulse buy from the nearby Walgreen's - winked at her. The prism in her vision was the only clue that she had been crying. She hadn't even realized it. Aislinn, as a rule, didn't cry. There wasn't much point, really. Not when it only signified a weakness. Not when there was no one there to hold you, or wipe the tears away, or offer some comforting words. When you were alone, and all was said and done, tears only depleted you of fluids that could be more useful elsewhere.

She had no family. No friends. No life. A status known in the Army as SNAFU – Situation Normal, All Fucked Up. It was right up there with FUBAR – Fucked Up Beyond All Repair.

The big clock tower a couple of blocks away chimed. Ten bells. Aislinn closed her eyes and let each one settle inside her, the noise somehow soothing. Only when the last one faded away did she open her eyes and screw the top back on the bottle of Jack.

Aislinn brushed her teeth and washed her face, avoiding the haunted hazel eyes she knew she would see if she looked in the mirror. She carefully combed her hair – long thick waves of caramel and mocha and dark chocolate and gold – now well past her shoulders. Stripping off the army-issue T and gym shorts, she slid into the nicest outfit she had – a pair of black jeans, black shirt, black boots with kick-ass heels. What the hell, she thought, glancing down at the ever-present dog tags. On top of them, Aislinn put on the white gold cross, the fine delicate chain feeling exceptionally light in her fingers. It matched the series of hoops and studs along her ears, her nipples, her navel, and her sex, the results of a whole lot of dares and *carpe diems*.

It was Christmas Eve, after all.

She tucked a few blades into her boots and at the small of her back. Strung some thin wire into her belt loops that could be used as a garrote in a pinch. Tucked a couple of six-point throwing stars and her personal favorite – the 4-pointed Cold 80SSA Heavy Sure Strikes – into the special custom double-lined pockets she'd sewn in herself. Then she donned her most prized possession – a black leather duster that clung to her frame like a lover and extended to mid-calf.

Her few remaining material possessions – the bottle of Jack, a dog-eared raggedy romance novel (for when she needed an escape), toothbrush and toothpaste, comb, pocket rocket (to be used in conjunction with the paperback), a roll of cash, and a change of clothes – were all stuffed into her small black leather pack and slung over her shoulder.

No matter what happened tonight, she already knew she wouldn't be returning to the seedy little rat trap she'd called home for the past couple of months.

Just because all "official" records listed her as honorably discharged didn't mean she wasn't still on active duty. War was still war. It didn't matter if it was fought in a jungle or a desert or a city of approximately eight million people, most of which didn't even have a clue they were one wrong step away from finding out. It was her job to keep it that way. Aislinn was a ghost, a shadow, a bump in the night that kept the other bumps at bay.

She attended midnight Mass first. *Why did they call it midnight Mass if it started at eleven*, she wondered, digging her hands deeper into her pockets and bracing herself against the bitter cold. It was just one of the thousands of innocuous little mysteries she pondered, but that really didn't matter at all. It sure as hell was easier to think about that than the deeper, darker stuff, though, so it was all good.

Instead of joining the others making their way up the aisle and filing into the pews, Aislinn remained in the back, hidden in the shadows behind one of the arched columns. God knew that she was there, and really, that was all that mattered. He was the only one who might have cared, but even that was questionable.

When the priest paused, beseeching the others to offer their own intentions before God, Aislinn bowed her head and closed her eyes.

Happy Birthday, Jesus.

She hastily added a few more words, the same Christmas wish she had been making in one form or another since she was old enough to understand the concept of wishes.

Aislinn slipped quietly out of the church ahead of the others as the last of the communion was being given, earning a disapproving glance or two from the suited guys in charge of the collection baskets. It was a sin to leave before the priest, one of her foster mothers once told her, a lesson that was later driven home by being forced to spend hours kneeling on bags of dried peas so she wouldn't forget. Yet Aislinn felt fairly confident that God would give her a pass on this one. Slipping out of Mass early paled in comparison to some of the other sins she had committed.

There was only one commandment, in fact, that Aislinn never even came close to breaking: *I, the Lord, am your God. You shall have no other gods besides me.* The others? Well… She had killed (in self-defense or in the defense of her unit). She had stolen (when her starving belly demanded it). She had coveted and lied and a host of other soul-damning no-no's, all loosely based on her shit life and a really strong survival instinct. Unfortunately for her, though, the ten commandments didn't come with exception clauses.

Besides, her premature departure from Mass was as much for the benefit of the smiling, happy parishioners as it was for her own. Aislinn didn't have any misconceptions about herself; she knew she made people uncomfortable. It wasn't just the clothes, though she *was* totally rocking the whole Underworld vibe. There was something about her, some aura of danger and death that had people averting their gazes and giving her a wide berth, sometimes going as far as to cross the street in blatant avoidance.

A lesser woman might have despaired, but not Aislinn. To despair meant that at some point, you had to have had some hope.

Silently, alone, Aislinn slipped through the streets, watchful and vigilant.

* * *

Lachlan Brodie cursed thrice more. "Where are they all bloody coming from?"

His small party of seven – himself, three of his six brothers, and three trusted clansmen - was returning from making the final arrangements for his upcoming betrothal. At thirty and two, it was high time to settle down and start breeding some heirs. He was the eldest son, after all, and as laird of Dubhain, it was his duty.

This particular match had been two years in the

making; Lachlan was nothing if not thorough. Elyse was a fine woman. Well-bred, she came from a good family that would add both land and coin to the Brodie holdings, not to mention that her father was a man of considerable influence. The fact that she stirred neither his heart nor his loins did not worry him overmuch. He had yet to meet a woman who did.

The attack had been unexpected, but Lachlan was not unprepared. Such things were not uncommon. Thanks to the work of his father and grandfather and more before him, Dubhain was a fine keep. Rich in resources and strategically placed, it was highly coveted, particularly among those who sought to reap the rewards others had sown with little or no effort beyond the brandishing of a well-placed sword.

He drew the claymore from where it sat along his back, the heavy weight of the long-sword familiar in his hand. Typically it was a two-handed weapon, but Lachlan had the superior strength and skill that allowed him to wield the blade effectively with one. His other hand clutched his favorite battle axe – a legacy from his father - while he directed his seasoned stallion with the slightest nudges of his knees and heels.

The others were already forming a defensive circle. As kinsmen, they had spent their entire lives training and fighting together; they instinctively knew the moves and methods of one another. It was unnecessary to give audible direction or shout out a plan. They had already orchestrated the moves in their own minds with astonishing synchronicity.

Seven men against two dozen plus. Some would think the odds were stacked against the Brodies, but they would be fools. Four-to-one was child's play for men of their skill and prowess. Not to mention that Lachlan's bloodline tended to create some of the largest men in the Highlands. At six-six and as broad as a stable door, Lachlan was considered "average" among the males in his clan. And he, like his whooping brethren, were itching for a good fight after behaving so well on this last journey.

But even big, skilled lairds can make mistakes when they grow overconfident. Hot on the tail of one cur who sought to flee, Lachlan followed him into the woods and unwittingly found himself in a small clearing, suddenly surrounded.

Chapter 2

Aislinn slowly returned to consciousness. Her eyes were heavy, her limbs like lead. For all intents and purposes, it felt like she was suffering the aftereffects of one hell of a bender, though she was not one to overindulge. As a rule, Aislinn liked to remain in complete control of her faculties, and would never willingly have made herself that vulnerable, especially not without her team to watch her six.

The errant thought slipped through the walls she'd erected around her heart and scored a direct hit before she could stop it.

You don't have a team anymore.

Before the survivor's guilt could gain full hold again, she forced those thoughts away, citing the mantra the Army shrink had made her repeat until she could almost believe it: There was nothing she could have done. Nothing anyone could have done. Bad shit happens.

So what the hell had happened this time? She tried to think back. She remembered leaving the church, walking up and down the streets, her feet taking her where she needed to be. Usually it was the bus station, or a train station, or the occasional dock - someplace where the criminal element thrived. Somewhere where it wasn't difficult to find someone who could benefit from her taxpayer-funded skills training and life experiences.

But she hadn't been drawn to any of the usual haunts. After wandering aimlessly for a while, she had cleared her mind and found herself moving toward the park. She must have circled the outer path twice before coming upon the pile of shivering rags huddled between the bench and the trees.

It wasn't the first time, and the odds were that it wouldn't be the last. There were too many like that. Too many homeless, too many addicts, too many who had no place to go and no one they could turn to for help.

She remembered reaching down to see exactly what she was dealing with when she felt the back of her head explode and everything went black...

Aislinn lifted her hand and gingerly touched the base of her skull, wincing when it shot a fresh wave of pain right through to her frontal lobe. Her fingers came away sticky and dark, which meant the wound was probably still bleeding a little, but it didn't seem to be life-threatening at least. She'd had a lot worse.

Thank God for small favors, she thought wryly.

She'd definitely had her bell rung, though, as evidenced by her current level of disorientation. Aislinn endeavored to push the pain and haze into the background and focus. Distraction was a good way to get herself killed. Or worse.

She could feel the grass beneath her and see the fuzzy outline of trees through her blurred vision, but it felt different somehow. It was no longer dark, she realized; maybe that's what was throwing her off. Exactly how long had she been out?

Her hands automatically went toward her weapons as she patted around her body. *All present and accounted for*, she thought, sighing with relief. Even her pack was still loosely slung over one shoulder.

She pushed herself up to sitting, closing her eyes while the world spun wildly around her and screwed with her senses.

It wasn't just the daylight that seemed incongruous. Aislinn didn't feel the biting cold as she should, either. Snow had already begun to fall in earnest during her last foray along the path, promising a white Christmas for the first time in years. But rather than finding herself face down on frozen ground, she was laying on what appeared to be soft – albeit uncut – grass. And it was *warm*.

The scents were all wrong, too. Snow had its own smell – anyone who spent any time up North knew that. But there was no hint of it now. Nor was there any discernable whiff of trash, dead leaves, or the ever-present aromas of stale beer and urine usually so prevalent in the park. She expanded her lungs, pleased when they didn't protest too much, and drew in the scents of grass, clean air, and oddly enough, something that smelled like dried herbs. Lavender, maybe, or heather.

Her senses were returning to her slowly but surely. As her hearing came back online and the annoying buzz faded, her brain struggled to identify the sounds. One was easy enough – men. Loud, bellowing men, grunting and spewing forth colorful vulgarities in a thick brogue.

And … horses? Not that she was particularly familiar with the beasts, but even she could recognize a few snorts and whinnies.

There was something else, too – a repeated, rhythmic clanging that resounded in her skull painfully and immediately roused her self-preservation instinct.

She rubbed at her eyes until the last of the little black dots faded away. And then shut them again quickly in disbelief. Clearly the blow to her head had caused significant damage, because there was no way what she had seen could be real. She decided she must be suffering from some kind of displaced psychosis resulting from a head injury and repeated viewings of *The Highlander* during late night bouts of insomnia.

She pinched herself – *hard* – then opened her eyes again, but the surreal scene hadn't faded. She tried again and caught her breath. *Yep. Still there.*

The more she watched – she had quite a vivid subconscious imagination, it seemed – the more entranced she became. Especially by the super-sized guy sporting the black and green plaid. A warrior, for sure, with his long, flowing auburn hair braided at the temples and a symphony of rippling muscles. With the face of an archangel – hard and masculine yet otherworldly beautiful, sinfully defined arms and legs, he moved with lethal grace and skill.

Despite his size and obvious proficiency in combat, he seemed to be a bit overwhelmed at that moment. Aislinn counted no less than six men attacking the warrior all at once. They, too, were large men sporting kilts, but they didn't have the same skill with a sword – *and holy shit, was that an axe?* - as the really big one, and the colors of their plaids were different.

The big guy was holding his own, she noted with no little amount of respect. But then a movement in her peripheral vision caught her attention. As Aislinn watched in growing horror, three more men emerged from the trees behind the warrior. With all of his focus on those in front of him and along his sides, he didn't see the threat as she did.

It's just a dream, she told herself, most likely the result of blunt-force head trauma. But before she could fully process that thought, she was on her feet, shoving her personal discomfort aside and stealthily moving toward the action as her training kicked in. It might be just a dream, but it was *her* dream, and she'd be damned if she'd allow such a fine warrior to go down by a sword to the back in any dream of hers.

Aislinn launched herself into the fray, pulling her blades from her boots as she did so. In a series of lightning fast kicks and spins, she took out the three men attacking her warrior from behind before they even knew what hit them. As the Mel Gibson look-alike turned around to see the commotion, she caught the flash of a sword sailing through the air – right at her warrior's head.

* * *

Lachlan could not believe his eyes. An avenging angel had appeared out of nowhere! She was yelling something to him, but he couldn't make out what it was. Then she was launching herself into the air, twisting her body as she did so. Her feet slammed hard against his chest, her momentum and the unexpected blow pushing him backwards, knocking him to the ground. He felt, rather than saw, the blade pass inches from his head on the way down only moments before he felt the soft weight of her body press down upon him, her feet near his shoulders and her head somewhere around his knees.

Though he distinctly heard the rush of breath from her lungs upon impact, the wee sprite did not hesitate for even a moment. She scrambled to her feet and grabbed for his sword, muttering foreign words when she found it too heavy to wield effectively.

As he attempted to gather his wits, she relinquished her hold upon the pommel and extracted her own small, sharp-looking weapons from her deep pockets as she straddled him protectively, flinging small shiny pointed disks with unerring precision at those creeping forward, hoping to attack him while he was down.

Lachlan looked up at the surreal creature atop him. Wild hair in streaks of darkest brown to near gold. Garbed in strange black cloth that hugged her so snugly that every feminine curve and dip was revealed.

"Well, dream warrior?" she asked, looking over her shoulder at him, grinning as if she was thoroughly enjoying herself. "Are you going to get up and help me or do I have to kick their asses all by my lonesome?"

Released from his reverie, he encircled her tiny waist with two large hands and lifted. A breath later, he sprung up beside her. He would attempt to puzzle out the strange visions afflicting him later; at that moment he had more immediate business to attend to.

"Behind me!" he commanded, shoving her and attempting to shield her with his much larger body.

"Screw that!" she answered, spinning to place her back to him. They fought back to back, circling as if they had trained together forever. In a series of mere minutes, all but two of the attackers lay still and unmoving, the others having fled for their lives.

With the threat nullified, Lachlan was able to turn his full attention to the mysterious creature that had appeared out of nowhere to render aid.

"Yer bleeding," Lachlan said, reaching out to touch the sprite.

"No shit, Sherlock," she murmured, leaping out of his reach gracefully.

"Doona fash, lass." Lachlan tried to soften his naturally deep, rumbling voice. "I just want te ken how badly ye are hurt."

"I'll live," she said, blowing a few strands of that magnificent mane out of her face as she surveyed the damage. "Friends of yours?"

For as fierce as she had been in battle, she was obviously skittish when not. He would not push – for now - but he found himself burning with questions and the need to touch her again, if only to make sure she was real. As long as she made no attempt to flee before he had a chance to do either, he could be patient.

"Nay," he said, punctuating the statement by using his foot to push one or two of the fallen onto their backs and peer down into their faces. "McCrae clan, by their colors."

As he tried to identify the rogues, he felt a sudden draft of air around his privates. He turned around quickly and caught the sprite lifting the back of his kilt with wide eyes and a wicked grin on her face. Shocked, Lachlan stepped away quickly. "What do ye think yer doing, lass?"

"I always wondered what a Scotsman wore under his kilt," she said unrepentantly in response to his glare.

"Impudent wench."

She narrowed her eyes. "Wench?" Then she laughed. It was a beautiful, clear sound, sending the strangest sensations into his chest. "I've been called worse, I suppose."

What kind of lass openly peeked beneath a man's kilt? Or wore trews? Or looked like an angel and fought like a Furie? Or – and this one gave him the most unease – made his body feel like it was filled with light whenever she flashed him a smile and looked at him with those exquisitely clear green and amber eyes?

Mayhap she was one of the legendary Valkyries they told stories of in the highest hills – women who appeared on the battlefield to determine which mortally wounded soldiers would live and which would die.

"What are ye?" he whispered roughly before he could stop himself.

Rather than be offended, as he feared she might, she appeared to consider his query.

"Hmmm. Good question. At the moment, I would say... *delusional* pretty much covers it. You know, concussion, possible cranial swelling, that sort of thing. Those Highlander romances must have really gotten to me," she murmured. "Gorgeous brawny Celts that can make a woman swoon just by…" She shook her head, wincing. "Nevermind. Why were those men trying to kill you?"

She'd answered him, but he had no idea what she'd actually said. She acted like he should understand, though, and he was hesitant to admit otherwise, lest it be seen as ignorance or weakness on his part. So he nodded and focused on her question instead.

"The same reason they all do," Lachlan said with a shrug. "They want my keep."

"Keep." She repeated the word as if it was unfamiliar to her, then her eyes opened wide. "You mean as in … a castle?"

"A modest one, aye," he answered warily, seeing the sudden gleam in her eye.

"So, are you like a lord or something?" she asked. Lachlan watched as she pulled her blades from the first couple of men, carefully wiping off the blood on their tartans before stowing the weapons away in hidden sheaths up and down the length of her wee form. She seemed totally unaffected, as if burying her blades in the hearts of men was an everyday occurrence. He told himself it would be good to remember that.

Of course, she didn't seem to be openly hostile to *him*. With her skill and speed, she could have buried one of those wee blades in him when he'd been foolish enough to turn his back on her a couple of minutes earlier. Instead she'd just peeked up his kilt. And, judging by her expression when he caught her, had liked what she'd seen. Blood rushed southward into his nether regions, filling a cock that had already begun to harden at the sight of her in all that form-fitting black.

But wait – she had asked him a question, hadn't she?

"Aye, a laird."

"Too cool."

Lachlan's brows drew together. The afternoon felt pleasantly warm to him.

The sound of horses reached their ears, along with shouts. "Oy! Lachlan! Ye alright?"

"Aye," Lachlan called back, watching with fascination as the female assumed a battle-ready stance. She looked gloriously fierce. Her legs were set slightly wider apart than her womanly hips and offset for optimal balance, a small blade in one hand and some kind of flat, semi-circular object with spikes in the other.

She poised, unnaturally still, her eyes the only things moving as she followed the sounds and pinpointed their locations. Suddenly she spun and her hand flew out. Lachlan only just managed to stop her before she buried the blade in his brother's heart.

"'Tis my kinsmon. Doona harm him."

She looked at the big hand encircling her wrist, then up at him with wide, shocked eyes. He barely managed to catch her before she went limp.

Chapter 3

Word of the minor skirmish spread quickly throughout the keep, but the real news was the unconscious woman the laird held to his chest as he rode through the gates. By the time Lachlan carried her to the guest chambers, his six younger brothers were already gathered around him.

After assuring them that the blood on his shirt was not his, they turned their attention to the strangely-clad female laid out atop the covers.

"Who is she, then?" Malcolm asked, studying her warily as if she might suddenly leap from the bed and attack. "From whence has she come? What business has she at Dubhain?"

"I doona ken," Lachlan said, brushing the hair back from her face so he could press a cool cloth against her forehead. He cleaned and dressed the open gash on the back of her head. The bleeding had all but stopped, but head wounds could be tricky. For now, all they could do was wait and see.

A cursory examination had shown no indication of any other injury that would justify the removal of her garments. He had managed to get the leather cloak off of her, but her form-fitting garb revealed more than Lachlan thought was proper in a room of seven men, so he draped her still form with a bedsheet, ensuring that the most provocative of areas were covered.

"That tricky little McCrae bastard led me straight inte a trap a beardless lad would have seen. 'Twas an ambush. The lass appeared out of nowhere, taking out three men at my back with her wee blades afore I even kenned they were there."

Their shock was evident, but not one of them even considered that their brother was lying or even exaggerating. Lachlan Brodie did neither.

"Beautiful *and* deadly?" mused Conall, his arms crossed over his broad chest. "I think I am in love. Is she Fae, do ye think?"

"No' likely," piped up Simon from where he sat at the foot of the bed. He seemed particularly fascinated with Aislinn's heeled boots, running the pads of his fingers along the silver rivets. "Fae wouldnae bleed so, would they?"

"Ye would think no'," Bowen murmured in agreement.

"She is a wee thing, though," observed Aengus, his eyes running the length of her. To demonstrate his point, he lifted up her limp hand and held it against his own. When he curled his fingers, they completely enveloped hers.

Lachlan did not care for the way his brothers were eyeing the lass, the way they were touching her, even less. "Wee, but fierce and quick enough te have almost buried her blade in yer chest."

Aengus heard the subtle warning and released Aislinn's hand, taking half a step back.

"Did she speak te ye, Lachlan?" asked Gavin.

"Aye, but I can no' make heads nor tails of most of it. She addressed me as someone called Sherlock. Do ye ken any such mon? Mayhap a traveler or visiting laird?"

They all thought for a moment and shook their heads. "What else did she say?"

"Weel, 'twas hard te make out, as I said. She does no' have the brogue, speaking more in the manner of an English, and she used some words I dinnae ken. At one point, though, I believe she was babbling on about delusions and romance and braw Scotsmen," he said, feeling the color rise to his cheeks when he recalled how she had lifted his kilt. There was no need to share that with them just yet, if at all.

Aislinn moaned softly, shifting slightly. Lachlan's weight on the side of the bed made her body pitch toward his.

"I think she might be coming 'round…"

With the exception of Lachlan, they all moved back.

* * *

The rumble of deep male voices intruded on the lovely dream she was having. She was in the

Highlands, fighting kilted warriors and kicking major ass. She smiled as she remembered the big one, the one with the amazing green eyes and biceps the size of her waist. In her fantasy, she had lifted his kilt and discovered one extremely well-hung Scot.

When she dreamed, she dreamed *big*.

She was just getting to the good part – the ripped Scot had just reached out and snatched her around the wrist, no doubt intending to ravish her in the fallowed grass as the adrenalin had them both pretty jacked-up – when the dream cut out. Talk about bad timing. Why couldn't whatever had woken her have just waited a few more minutes?

Aislinn cracked open her eyes and instantly realized she was not alone. In the sudden and full-scale fight-or-flight mode that came from serving nearly six consecutive twelve-month terms in the United States Army, the last four of which had her stationed with an elite Ranger unit, Aislinn scrambled back on the bed as far as she could. She reached for her blades, but they were gone.

"What did you do to me?" she asked, the menace in her voice interlaced with a fear she could not completely hide. "Where are my weapons?"

"Relax, lass," one guy said, and – *holy shit!* – it was the guy from her dream!

He spoke in what was surely meant to be a soothing voice, holding out his arms to show he had no weapons, but there was absolutely nothing *soothing* about him. He was pure, unadulterated alpha-male. *In a kilt.*

"We will no' harm ye, I give ye my word on that."

The sharp pain at the back of her skull sure felt real enough. "What does your word mean to me?" she demanded hotly. "You could be a pathological liar or a psychopath for all I know."

His expression turned instantly stormy. "Doona insult my honor in my own home," he warned in his booming voice.

"Fine. Give me my stuff and I'll get right the fuck out."

"Ye will no' be going anywhere," Lachlan said, standing firmly. "Not until ye tell us who ye are and how ye came te be on Brodie land."

"Who's going to stop me?" she smirked, all traces of fear now gone. That's what usually tended to happen when people tried to start telling her what she could and couldn't do, or worse, thought to intimidate her. They soon discovered that Aislinn was not a woman easily cowed, especially not by oversized alpha-male types. They fell the hardest of all.

"You?" Her eyes twinkled in challenge. His narrowed, piercing her with their intensity.

"Aye. An' if yer thinking te get past me, ye might want te take a good look around ye, lass."

The kilted warrior stepped his big frame aside, and several others came into view. Six, to be exact.

All bearing similar features to her dream guy and wearing the same colors, but varying slightly in eye color, hair color, age, and size. Six gorgeous men, muscled arms crossed over broad chests, wearing the same green and black plaid. And they were all staring at her as if she was some rare kind of bug.

Aislinn was swift and skilled, but she was not stupid. A quick assessment revealed only one exit, and it was behind all that prime male flesh. In this small space, made even more so by the hulking brutes now surrounding her, she would not be able to get past all of them, especially as she was unarmed.

Then she realized she didn't have to.

She pried herself away from the wall and eased back onto the bed with a big smile. "Right! My dream! It must be one of those weird ones, when you *think* you're awake, but you're really not. I'm in a coma, and you all are just creations of my overactive and obviously sex-starved imagination."

The men looked at each other, bemused. The big guy finally said, "Ye think ye are dreaming?"

"Well of course I am!" she said brightly. "And doing a fine job of it, if I do say so myself. I wonder if this is how Hannah Howell comes up with ideas for her novels…"

"Mayhap she is a wee bit touched," the youngest looking one said quietly, tapping his temple.

"You mean crazy?" she laughed, drawing a

small circle in the air beside her temple. "Yeah, I'm sure some people think so, but this is probably more of an NDE type of thing – you know, a Near Death Experience. I've had them before, but never like this. Or I guess it could be a total mental breakdown - which means the blow to the head I took was a lot worse than I thought and I'm probably not going to last the night. But if that means I get to live out what little time I have left surrounded by fierce, gorgeous Highland warriors, I can't think of a better way to go."

She leaned over and touched the hem of the one closest to her, intending to lift it. Shocked, he took a step back and slapped her hand away.

"Touchy," she pouted. "But I guess it wouldn't be any fun if it were too easy. The men in the books are always a little reluctant at first, but they eventually come around."

The big guy – he was clearly the leader – frowned. "Ye were attacked? Ere ye came here?"

"Yep. Fucker came up behind me – kind of like those asshats tried to do to you earlier – but I didn't have anyone watching my six. Hey – that might explain some of this. My mind couldn't accept the fact that I'd die from such a cowardly act, so I created this whole scenario to compensate. Right now I'm probably lying in a hospital bed somewhere, and God's finally taking some pity on me. Or, hell, maybe I'm still in the park and some homeless guy is pissing on me even as we speak."

"I see what ye mean," said the one who had slapped her hand. "She does no' speak like any lass I have ever heard."

"She took a mighty blow te the head, dinnae she?" whispered another.

"Aye. And she did lose a lot of blood."

"What?" Aislinn touched the back of her head, then flashed a smug smile. "No biggie. You should see the other guys."

"Now doona fash, lass, we will no' hurt ye, but we need te ken if ye have other injuries."

She grinned and waggled her index finger at him. "Naughty Celt. You just want me to take my clothes off. Why didn't you just say so?"

Aislinn pulled her top up and over her head, revealing her favorite satiny black bra. Functional yet sexy, it gave her the support she needed while managing to make her feel pretty good about herself in the process. Soldier she might be, but she was also a woman.

Apparently it had a positive effect on big, brawny males too. As one, their eyes opened wide and they sucked in a collective breath. She reached to the front clasp to undo that, too, but before she could, the big one grabbed his plaid and threw it over her. In his haste, it covered not only the parts she had nearly exposed, but her entire body as well.

"What in the devil's name are ye thinkin', lass?"

She laughed, pulling the plaid down from her

face. "Gonna pretend to be shy, are we? I doubt I have anything you haven't already seen. You romance novel types are always well-experienced in pleasing a woman. In Hannah's books, the *lads* usually start, uh, *tupping* the tavern maids around the age of fourteen or so, am I right?"

Without waiting for them to respond – their shock seemed to have rendered them temporarily mute - she tapped her teeth with her glossy black nail and regarded each of them carefully. "So… given that you are all probably at least in your twenties, and being that you are sinfully delicious, I would guess that you are all well-versed in the female anatomy."

"Out!" the clearly panicked laird commanded the others, even as he was stepping backwards. "I will send Old Meg in te help ye," he managed before he slammed the door behind him, leaving a laughing Aislinn alone in the room.

* * *

Lachlan found the motherly woman puttering around the kitchens, just as she had been doing for as long as he could remember. Old Meg had been around when his Da had been but a lad. No one knew exactly how old she was, and they weren't stupid enough to ask. The quiet woman was a force of nature, thought of by Lachlan and his brothers as more of a favorite aunt than a servant.

After explaining the situation, she had nodded and assured Lachlan she would see to their new guest, then left to arrange for a bath and a change of clothing.

"She is unlike anything I have ever seen," breathed Malcolm as they regrouped in the Great Hall. "Do ye ken who she is?"

"Nay," Lachlan said, downing his ale before it even hit the table, trying to get the images of her creamy-looking skin and decidedly lush, barely-covered breasts out of his mind. He drank another down right after. "She appears to think that she is caught in some kind of a dream. She does no' believe any of this – any of *us* – are real."

And apparently, she didn't think particularly highly of them, either. At least not at first. He hadn't recognized all of the words she had spewed at him, but he did hear "liar" clearly enough and assumed some of the others were just as derogatory.

In retrospect, he probably should not have raised his voice to her as he had, not when she had backed herself into a corner and hissed at him like some frightened, feral kitten.

"But how can that be?"

Lachlan was asking himself the same question.

"The lass is clearly addled," offered Aengus. "And 'tis no surprise, given the bump ye found on her noggin."

"More than a bump," Lachlan corrected. "It looked like someone tried to bash in her wee skull with a cudgel." He shook his head wondering for the dozenth time how she could have stayed upright, let alone fought like a right Furie with such a wound.

"I heard rumor of a young lass disappearing up north no' so long ago," Conall mused. "From what I recall, this lass would be about the right age."

"Ye think it might be her?"

"Might be," Conall shrugged. "She had te come from somewhere, dinnae she? I think if she was from anywhere around here, one of us would have remembered her." He grinned. "She is no' the sort of lass a mon easily forgets."

Lachlan scowled, unsure why he suddenly found his brother's lascivious grin so irksome. They were a randy bunch, to be sure, but it had never struck a nerve before.

"See if ye can discover more about this missing lass."

Before anyone could comment further, a scream rent the air. Lachlan and the others rushed toward the guest quarters only to find Old Meg barreling out of the room, her hand clutched to her chest and her face as pale as the silvery moon.

"Meg, what is it?"

The old woman's hand came up to her mouth and she shook her head, her eyes wild, before wrenching free of Lachlan's grasp and scurrying down the hall.

Dreading what he might find, Lachlan opened

the door very slowly, keeping himself between whatever was in there and his brothers. He was the one who had brought the addled female into the keep; he would bear the responsibility for her.

He looked around, half-expecting to find a crazed Furie, or at least the room in shambles given the intensity of Meg's shriek, but all he saw was the female, perched calmly upon the rim of the bathing tub, her back to him.

Naked.

He slammed the door shut behind him, barking orders for the others to tend to Meg and return to the Great Hall. Ignoring their protests, he turned, leaning his bulk against the door in case any of them thought to disobey.

The first thing he noticed were the swirls of black between her shoulder blades, an intricate and ancient Celtic design of incredible beauty etched into her very skin. As were the bands of interwoven knots along her upper arms. The dark black ink was crisscrossed with irregular white lines.

Scars.

Warrioress... the word echoed in his mind.

Then his gaze went lower, following the natural curve of her waist and the flair of womanly hips...

The sprite tossed him an amused look over her shoulder. "Sorry about that. Didn't mean to scare her. I'm guessing women don't normally shave in your time, huh?"

Only then did he notice the glint of the straight

blade in her hand. Where had she gotten *that*? She was running it skillfully up and down her legs, despite the fact that her eyes remained on him.

"I probably should have done this before I left – the whole clean underwear theory and all that - but *really*. Only I could create a fantasy world in which I still had to *shave*."

Incapable of speech, he watched, mesmerized, as she moved the blade from ankle to knee, then rinsed it in the water and repeated the motion. She did the same along her thighs, moving more swiftly than he thought was advisable, but the woman seemed unconcerned.

He couldn't completely contain the choking noises that came from his throat, however, when she spread her legs and leaned forward, the slight, quick movements of her arms suggesting much smaller strokes. While she was still turned away from him, he couldn't see exactly what she was doing, but his mind conjured the images for him.

And then, *sweet and merciful Savior*, she set the blade aside and dipped her lithe little body into the tub. When she rose and turned toward him, her lightly bronzed skin was wet and gloriously smooth. Lachlan had never seen anything like it. The slight glinting of metal captured his gaze, hung around her neck and nestled in her cleavage. He swallowed hard when he saw similar adornments in her breasts and navel.

"Yes," she said, answering his unspoken

question, the amusement evident in her voice when she followed his eyes southward. "I've got one there, too."

Suddenly Lachlan felt as if he could no longer draw breath. Without a word, he opened the door and stepped out into the hallway, pale and shaken.

"Weel?" said his brothers, trying to glimpse into the room, but Lachlan's large frame wouldn't allow it. "Is everything alright?"

Lachlan turned stricken eyes on them. "No," he rasped.

It might never be alright again.

He ushered them away from the door and back toward the Great Hall, forcing himself to follow along behind them. There were very few things that left Lachlan Brodie feeling as if he had been cold-cocked upside the head with the business end of a claymore. Seeing a wet, naked lass, flushed and completely hairless from the neck down was one of them.

Lachlan groaned and clenched his hands into tight fists with the nearly uncontrollable urge to run his fingers over all that pristine, smooth flesh. Or better yet, to taste it as he laved his tongue over every exquisite inch.

He would pay particular attention to those areas of the flesh decorated with ancient Celtic designs, symbols that added a particularly heated draw, for they very clearly marked her as one of his own. Add in the delicate, flashing silver and diamond adornments upon her most womanly parts, and his cock literally grew wet with anticipation.

Never mind the fact that she was quite possibly the most beautiful woman he had ever seen.

Or that she had saved his life.

It took every bit of self-control he had to walk away from that door and back toward the Great Hall where his brothers would undoubtedly want to know what had vexed Old Meg so and left him feeling shaken and a bit addled himself.

And what, exactly, was he going to tell them?

Chapter 4

"Oh, *hell* no," Aislinn breathed, picking up the gown with two fingers of each hand, holding it up and away as if it might bite her. The older woman had literally flung the dress onto the bed and fled as if Aislinn was the daughter of the devil himself. That didn't bother Aislinn in the least; she'd stopped worrying about what other people thought of her a long time ago.

But this was… not doable. The only time Aislinn had ever worn dresses had been long, long ago, when the social workers had insisted upon it. It was important, they'd said, to make a good impression on potential foster families.

And look how well *that* turned out.

There was just so much of it. Even if she could figure out which end was up, there was no way she was going to put that thing on. She guessed that the laird was trying to be accommodating, and she really didn't want to offend him, but she was only willing to take things so far. Besides, she reasoned, this was *her* dream. She could do whatever the hell she wanted.

With that in mind, she carefully draped the

gown over the high back of the chair and extracted her extra set of clothes from her pack – camo cargos and a black tank. Liberally applying some deodorant, she drew her hair up into a ponytail. She brushed her teeth, amazed at how such a simple act could make her feel so much better. Then she hand-washed her blood-stained clothes in the leftover bath water and draped them over the sill to dry.

Poor man, thought Aislinn with a chuckle as she remembered the look on the laird's face when he'd come in and seen her in the bath. Even in this bizarre dream world she felt it safe to assume he'd never seen anything like her before. Then again, she was shaving and doing laundry in her dream-fantasy, so who was she to judge?

And, honestly, she had never seen anything quite like him before, either. Her body grew uncomfortably warm just thinking about him. About the laser-like intensity of those eyes. Of the sense of barely-leashed power held in check. All those delicious, rippling muscles. And, dear Lord, the man had a derriere to weep for.

She shook her head. All of them were gorgeous, really. But it was only the *laird* who made her heart beat faster, made her most feminine of parts tingle. Too bad it wasn't real. Then again, creating fantasies was kind of a specialty of hers, a craft finely honed deep inside the mind of a little girl whose reality sucked ass on the best of days.

Aislinn reached into her bag and pulled out the

small black velvet pouch containing her miniature BFF. "Hello, old friend," she said softly.

A knock at the door startled her; she dropped the pouch and the little silvery device rolled out, right in front of the large feet of the man who stepped over the threshold. Thankfully, he didn't seem to notice. His brows drew together as he took in her outfit, then glanced over and saw the gown draped across the bed. "The frock does no' please ye?"

"It's beautiful, really," she said, hoping she didn't sound too ungrateful. "But I'm not really a dress kind of girl."

"Nay?" he asked on a breath, making that one word sound way more passionate than it should have. "I dinnae ken there was such a thing."

She shrugged, suddenly feeling very small and way too hot. Was it possible that he had grown in the past few hours since she'd last seen him? Instead of cowering (or sighing), however, she drew in a breath and faced him head-on. Playing the submissive just wasn't in her genes, no matter how much her overzealous hormones protested.

"I bet there are a lot of things about me that you never *kenned*."

A slight blush rose in Lachlan's cheeks, the hint of a shy, boyish smile dancing at the corners of his very grown-up, very masculine lips. It easily took ten years off his face, made him all but irresistible.

"You should do that more often," Aislinn said, the knowledge that this was all a dream making her daring. "Smile, I mean. You're beyond gorgeous as it is, but when you smile, it's positively devastating."

Was it her imagination, or did his chest puff out a little at her words? Surely women said things to him like that all the time; the guy probably had to beat them off with a stick.

Except there weren't any other women in her fantasy. Just him. And her. In her room. Alone.

"Not many lasses would be bold enough to say so," he pointed out in that deep, rumbling voice. Internally, some of her muscles rippled right along with it. She tightened her abs and did a few Kegels in an effort to make it stop.

"My point *exactly*," she said with a smile and a wink. She nodded toward the bundle in his hands. "So tell me what it is you have there."

"Och, aye. I thought ye might be a wee bit hungry." Lachlan lifted the lid of the large, hand-woven basket and the most delicious aromas filled the room. "Ye slept through the evening repast, but Old Meg managed te assemble a decent enough meal for ye." He stepped forward, unknowingly kicking her little silver pocket rocket beneath the bed as he did so.

Aislinn blinked, nonplussed. If he had drawn a weapon or threatened her, she would have taken it all in stride, her shields always raised and ready.

But his kindness was wholly unexpected, and therefore, caught her off-guard.

People were not generally kind to her. Fought with her, tried to control or take advantage of her, yes. Avoided her – check. But provide her with clothing and food with no ulterior motive?

It was a dream, sure, but some life lessons were pretty hardwired into her brain. In her nearly twenty-five years on this planet – dream state or not – she could probably count on one hand the number of times a man reached out to her without the intent to hurt, debase, or punish her in some fashion.

For a moment she considered the possibility that he had drugged or poisoned the food, but her instincts told her otherwise, and Aislinn had learned to always trust her instincts.

"That's very kind of you, uh, …" Aislinn frowned, realizing she didn't even know his name.

"Lachlan," he provided, placing the basket down upon the small table beside the fireplace. "Lachlan Brodie, at yer service." He bowed low at the waist, surprising her. She recognized it for what it was – a great sign of trust on his part.

"Lachlan Brodie," she murmured, tasting the name. It, like everything else about him, left a very pleasant taste in her mouth. "It suits you. Pleased to meet you, Lachlan Brodie. My name is Aislinn McKenna."

Lachlan bowed again, this time taking her hand in his and bringing it to his lips. "And I, ye,

Mistress McKenna." His eyes glimmered with something unreadable. "Am I correct in assuming ye are no' spoken for?"

His words sent a momentary wave of sadness over her. Spoken for? As in claimed, or even wanted? The idea would have been laughable if it wasn't so pathetic. Clearly he had no idea who he was talking to.

Aislinn caught her breath at the feel of his lips on the back of her hand. She sure as hell wasn't going to enlighten him. "You are correct, Mr. Brodie."

"Mayhap 'tis too familiar a request, but would ye call me by my given name?" he asked. "I like the way it sounds when ye speak it."

"I will. In case you haven't noticed," she said with a sly grin, "I'm not particularly fond of following everyone else's rules, *Lachlan*."

He might like hearing it, but she liked saying it. She didn't even try to mimic his pronunciation; if she tried to recreate the hard, guttural sound, it would probably come off more like she was trying to hack up a hair ball. So she softened the hard "k" sound and, on a whim, added a lilting little roll in the middle.

Hey, it was her dream. If she wanted to say his name like it made her wet (which it kind of did), then she would.

"May I address ye as Aislinn, then?" he asked almost shyly. "I ken 'tis not a proper request but…"

"I would like that very much," she replied before he could finish. Proper had never been her style, and the way he said it felt... intimate.

With only inches separating them – and Lachlan still holding her hand – the room grew very warm very quickly.

"Have you eaten yet?" she asked suddenly.

"Nay."

"Will you join me then?"

He smiled, and once again, the result was devastating. "I would be honored te break bread with ye, Aislinn. Thank ye."

* * *

Lachlan was glad that he had not had much of an appetite when he'd gone down to the Great Hall earlier. His belly, it seemed, had been a bit unsettled, and he had managed only a pint of ale and a few bites of bread and cheese. Sharing a private meal with his intriguing guest was definitely preferable to thinking about her from the other side of the keep while listening to his brothers theorize on her or her purpose.

"This is amazing. What is it?" After a mouth-wateringly delicious meal of roasted meat, potatoes and coarse, dark bread, Lachlan had revealed a covered bowl filled with fresh berries and a thick white topping that had Aislinn's eyes lighting up.

"Cream sweetened with honey," he replied,

wondering vaguely where she might be from that she was not familiar with cream, while at the same time making a mental note to have lots more of it on hand. Watching her take such pleasure from it was an unpredictably arousing experience.

"Mmmm," Aislinn said, licking the back of the spoon (which did absolutely nothing to temper his untoward and lustful reaction). "I don't think I've ever had real cream before. The fake stuff can't compare."

It was one more thing she said that Lachlan did not understand. How could one "fake" cream? Yet there was nothing remotely dishonest in the way she spoke of such things. It only increased his desire to know more about this fascinating female, as well as his desire to experience first-hand the masterful strokes of that wicked wee pink tongue.

"Tell me about yer life, Aislinn," Lachlan asked, taking a spoonful of berries and cream from the bowl and holding it to her lips. As much as he loved the dessert, he enjoyed her pleasure even more. He had a feeling that would extend to many other things as well. The vexing lass lit a fire in his blood by doing nothing more than partaking of a simple meal.

"Why?" she asked. She wrapped her slim fingers firmly around his wrist, a silent warning in case he entertained the thought of taking back his spoon before she had finished. That made him smile. Her skin felt wonderfully warm against his;

he would feed her the rest like this if only to keep her touching him.

"I have never met anyone like ye. I am curious."

Her lids lowered to half-staff and she released his hand. He could feel her pulling away from him, the brief – and he guessed rare – easy rapport between them fading rapidly. The softness of her features schooled into something slightly harder. He did not care for it at all.

"I don't want to talk about that. This is my dream. Let me enjoy it."

"What if 'tis no' a dream?" Lachlan asked, immediately regretting the words the moment they passed over his lips. Instead of distancing herself further, however, she completely surprised him with a dazzling smile.

"It has to be," she insisted. "Want to know how I know?"

He nodded, intrigued by her ability to go from one extreme to the other with so little effort. It was the sign of a woman who held great passion in her heart. He had already witnessed her fearlessness in battle, her boldness in word and deed, and her ability to express her pleasure with a radiance that rivaled that of the sun, so it was not wholly unexpected.

Aislinn shifted a little, so that her thigh pressed lightly against his. She didn't seem to notice, but he could scarcely think past the heat seeping into his flesh from the contact.

"Because in *my* life, people don't live in castles or keeps. The air is not pure and clean, food doesn't taste this good, and men like you don't exist. And if they did, they sure as hell wouldn't even notice someone like me."

If he had not been watching so closely, he might have missed the momentary flash of pain in her eyes, but it was gone just as quickly as it had come.

"How could a mon no' notice ye?" Lachlan said, honestly bemused. "The fool would have te be deaf, dumb, and blind!"

Aislinn's delicate features softened. "See? That's what I'm talking about. No flesh and blood man would ever think of saying something that sweet. Not to me."

Lachlan didn't know what to say. As he rolled her words around in his head, she added quietly, "I like your world a lot better."

There was very little about his unexpected guest that made sense to him. The way she spoke, the way she dressed, her lethal skills – they all confounded him. But if there was one thing Lachlan did know quite well, it was human nature. His ability to read people below the surface was but one of the things that made him such an excellent and fair laird.

After spending a few uninterrupted hours with the mercurial Aislinn McKenna, he was quite sure of two things. One - for all of her peculiarities, the woman had a good soul and the heart of a warrior. And two – that she was more accustomed to cruelty than kindness.

The first provided a sense of relief and appealed to his sense of honor and fair play. The second evoked a more visceral reaction from the male in him. Warrioress she might be, but she was still a female, and one who had known far too much pain.

She hadn't told him these things, of course. She hadn't really told him anything at all about herself, having skillfully avoided his personal questions and turning them back upon him. No, Lachlan had formed his opinions on things much more telling: the way she held herself, the emotion in her eyes in those rare moments when she let her control slip, the tone and timbre of her voice. That she had known abuse was evident in all of it.

It was in the way she had stumbled when she realized he had brought her food. In the almost shyly-posed request for him to join her in a meal. In the way she had savored each and every bite as though she did not know when she would have the chance to eat again.

Aislinn McKenna, Lachlan decided as he wished her a pleasant eve and returned to his quarters, definitely warranted further study.

Chapter 5

Aislinn was mildly surprised when the door opened so easily. Though Lachlan had never implied that she was a prisoner of any kind, she half-expected it to be locked or bolted. If the situations were reversed, and she suddenly found a warrior like Lachlan in her world, it's what she would have done, as much for his protection as everyone else's. Then again, there was no accounting for the rationality of dreams. She had to keep reminding herself of that, no matter how real things seemed.

She peeked out into the corridor, smiling when she saw the young boy waiting for her. Aislinn guessed his age to be somewhere around thirteen or so, though he was already several inches taller than she was. He had the same glowing green eyes as Lachlan and his brothers, the same features that were devilishly mischievous now and would become roguishly handsome in a few years. She had spotted him from her window earlier, and asked him if he would be so kind as to bring a set of his clothes to her.

"Are you Lachlan's son?" she asked suddenly, the question spewing forth before she could stop it as she motioned for him to come into the room.

The boy gave her a roguish half-smile. "Nay. I'm Rory. Malcolm's bastard."

Surprise and shock must have shown in her eyes, because the boy laughed. "There are a lot of bastards, here," he confided smoothly. "Just no' any proper heirs."

She saw him eyeing the plate of honeyed oatcakes that had been delivered to her earlier that morning and offered him one. "And you're... okay with that?" she asked doubtfully.

"Oh, aye. We are weel cared for," he said with particular glee, his mouth stuffed near to capacity. "There are many who are no' so fortunate."

Something old and painful stirred inside of Aislinn, but she refused to acknowledge it. "What about your mothers?" she asked.

"Weel, most are only too glad te be rid of us. While siring many sons is a mark of a strong and virile mon, the women who bear us out of wedlock are no' thought upon so kindly, are they? The verra fact that we exist is as much a source of shame te them as it is pride te our sires." He shrugged. "And we want for nothin'," he continued, stuffing another oatcake into his mouth. "The Brodie take care of their own now, doona they?"

He swallowed and pointed at the small pile of clothes he'd brought. "What are ye goin' te do with them?"

"What?" she asked, her mind snapping back from where it was wandering amidst forbidden thoughts of many a maid well-taken by such conscientious Brodies. "Oh. They're for me. I'm going to wear them."

The lad's eyes grew huge. "Ye? Lasses doona wear breeches."

"*This* lass does."

A mischievous grin grew over his features. "I can see now why my uncles are so besides themselves," he laughed. "That alone is worth the beatin' I'll get for sneakin' inte yer chambers."

Aislinn went still. She hadn't considered the boy might get in trouble when she spotted him earlier and had called to him from her window asking him to bring her some clothes. "You didn't tell anyone, did you?"

"Doona fash, lass," he winked, unfazed. Aislinn wondered at how, at such a young age, the boy could be so charming. He would, undoubtedly, be breaking a lot of hearts in a few years. "I'll gladly take a beatin' and more if ye promise te strut through the Great Hall wearing my breeches whilst my uncles are breakin' their fast. Ye've got te give me a head start te round up my kin, though. They will no' be wanting te miss this."

Rory's grin was infectious. Aislinn suddenly felt a strong compulsion to partake of a little harmless mischief. She hadn't planned on making a show out of it; she'd just wanted comfortable clothing in which to do a little exploring. But this was simply too good an opportunity to pass up.

"It's a deal," she agreed. "But only if you swear not to tell anyone where I got them."

"Aye, an accord it is, then. Since ye are in such a generous mood, would ye perhaps see fit te give us a kiss then as weel?"

Aislinn laughed and pushed him out of the room. Before she closed the door, however, she granted his request with a peck on the cheek that had him turning several shades of red.

"Sweet Virgin Mother," Conall breathed, his eyes lifting from their morning meal at the scarred table. He was the first to spot Aislinn, but other heads quickly lifted at his words. Similar utterances rippled up and down the long tables.

While Rory's trews were about the right length for a pair of ankle-length leggings, they were intended for the skinny legs and hips of a young boy, not for Aislinn's petite but generous curves. Especially since she tucked the loose-fitting laced shirt into the waistband. The shirt was a bit loose in places and was a fairly heavy material, but incapable of completely hiding her assets. The fact that she hadn't laced it all the way left the swell of her breasts just visible over the top. In the get-up, she felt like a sexy pirate.

All conversation ceased. Hands froze in mid-air, poised over plates or grasping at half-raised tankards, every eye glued on her.

"Aislinn," Lachlan said, his voice choked. "Where did ye get those?"

"Do you like?" she said, turning around so he – and the others – could view her from all angles. It was only when she looked into his face again that she began to realize she might have crossed a serious line. The silence in the hall was absolute. Her grin faded and she stopped twirling.

Meal forgotten, Lachlan shot to his feet, his big chair scraping as loud as thunder in the absolute quiet. Even from several yards away, it was plain to see the flames in his eyes.

"You know what?" she said, taking a step back, acutely aware of the fact that in her haste to do mischief, she had neglected to strap on her personal armory. "I'm not so hungry anymore. I think I'm going to go… do something else."

Without waiting for a reaction, Aislinn made a hasty retreat. She wound her way back up to the room she had been given, taking the steps two at a time. She managed to stuff her still-damp clothes into her pack and strap on all of her little friends before she caught the glint of the silver orb near the edge of the bed. Going down on all fours, she reached beneath the frame and closed her hand around it. As she was extracting herself, she turned and came face to face with a pair of overly large boots.

How could a man that big move that fast and make no sound to broadcast his approach?

Like some animated cartoon character, Aislinn gulped audibly as her gaze continued to rise into the powerful glare of Laird Lachlan Brodie. Over the course of her lifetime, she had come up against all sorts of authoritative men, good and bad alike; but she had never, *ever* felt the kind of raw, primal intensity currently emanating from this man.

Still, she would not cower before anyone. *Ever*.

She stood slowly, straightening to her full height so that she was staring at his breastbone, just inches from her face. Aislinn tried to keep her breaths steady and even as his heat and scent surrounded her.

Lachlan looked at the pack in her hands, then back into her face. "Thinkin' te leave, are ye?" His voice was lethally quiet, like a lover's whisper, made of fire and coated in ice.

Aislinn squared her shoulders. "I thought I might."

"Are ye in such a hurry te flee, lass?"

Yes. No. A few moments ago, Aislinn's only thought was to run, to find some quiet, out of the way place where she could pull her shit together and figure this all out. But where would she go? Sure, her subconscious must have created this place, drawing from bits and pieces of historical romance novels and late night cable television, but her conscious mind felt completely out of its element.

Everything here felt so *real*. She already knew she could experience pain, hunger, and an uncomfortable need to seek out the facilities, so she didn't doubt discomfort was part of the package. As a matter of fact, everything seemed the same except for the setting itself. It was as if she had simply been plucked out of one place and time and dropped into another.

Which was impossible.

The why and how of it didn't really matter, though. It was what it was, and Aislinn had learned a long time ago to deal with whatever curveballs life threw her way.

All things considered, this wasn't so bad. Real or not, at least she had a roof over her head and food she didn't have to catch or dig up on her own. And her finely-honed instincts told her that despite how intense these guys were, they wouldn't hurt her; there had already been plenty of opportunities to do so had they been so inclined.

Who knew how long this crazy dream was going to last? Didn't it make more sense to hang out here if she could, assuming she hadn't royally pissed off the laird and he'd come to kick her irreverent ass out?

And good Lord, she thought, getting a nice, up close and personal view of that broad chest, but was the man smacked together! Each inhale brought the scent of clean, fresh male into her lungs, making all of her other parts envious, wishing they had some of him in them, too.

She re-squared off her shoulders and centered her weight. The movement was slight, but obvious.

"Maybe," she sniffed.

One corner of Lachlan's mouth quirked. "Ye would no' make it te the gates dressed like that." His voice was rougher than normal. Husky. And sexy as all hell.

"Oh?" she asked, clenching the series of internal muscles that started somewhere between her legs and extended up into her rib cage. "And why is that?"

He stepped forward, crowding her, a wall of solid mass and muscle. There was no going through him. Reflexively, she stepped back. It was only when the back of her knees hit the bed frame and her butt hit the mattress that she realized she had nowhere to go. Great. Now she was looking straight at his crotch. And *damn*.

"Because. Ye'll have every mon that sees ye so wild with lust he will no' be able te help himself. Is that what ye want, Aislinn? Is that why ye have wrapped yourself in a package of temptation no mon can possibly resist?"

Wow. As if his words weren't enough to steal her breath, the sensual way he spoke them created a veritable vacuum in her chest.

"You seem to be doing just fine," she said bravely, but she wondered. Her instincts were telling her that Lachlan was leashing himself. And that thought was exciting. He didn't seem like the type of man who often warred with self-control.

He grinned at that, a smile so sexually charged that she actually felt herself grow wet, neither confirming nor denying the statement. She swallowed and clenched the object in her hand all that much more tightly.

"What have ye there?" he asked, his gaze drawn to the whitening knuckles of her fist. His eyes narrowed, no doubt wondering if she held one of her weapons.

"Nothing."

* * *

Her response was too quick, too... false. Lachlan's nostrils flared as he clearly sensed the lie. He was correct in his initial assessment; the woman was basically honest, even the tiniest lie to pass her lips as obvious as the pretty crimson flush now rising beneath her jawline.

Something about the wee female lit a fire in his blood and had every last nerve tingling. She might think she had a choice in the matter, but she didn't, not until he had some answers.

And until he had the chance to map out and taste every last delectable curve revealed by those garments.

His big hand came over hers, while his other

pried at her fingers. Fierce she might be, but she was no match for his superior strength.

He extracted the smooth, silvery object and looked at it warily. Oblong, much smaller than a hen's egg, it reflected the morning sunlight. He turned it this way and that, examining it with curiosity, startled when it vibrated to life in his hand.

His eyes widened as he closed his hand around it. "Is it a weapon?"

The crimson flush turned brilliant and extended up into her cheeks. "Um, no."

"Ye will tell me what this is." A demand.

"It's, um…" Aislinn looked everywhere except at him – the walls, the ceiling, the fireplace - "… a device a woman uses to give herself pleasure."

The temperature in the room shot up at least ten degrees. Most of it was due to the heat now radiating from his body, as the fire in his blood exploded into a raging inferno. He glared at her for several long moments, trying to gain purchase over the flames before they destroyed him and everything else around him.

When he spoke again, his voice was little more than a growl. "Ye will show me."

"I don't think so." Aislinn licked her lips nervously, yet he saw the desire there, too. Her cheeks were flushed, her eyes shining with arousal. He flicked his eyes downward, feeling a flare of triumph when he saw the hard tips of her breasts straining against the cloth.

"I am no' askin', lass." He thrust his hand out, opening his fingers. "Ye will do this for me."

* * *

Hands shaking, she took the device from his palm. It retained the heat of his hand, a fact that had her tightening her legs together. Was she actually considering this? Could she really do this?

There was some part of her that was thrilled by the idea of using the toy to alleviate some of the heavy need that she was feeling in his presence. To have him watch her while she did.

So why was she hesitating? This was her dream, damn it! For some reason she seemed to keep forgetting that. If she wanted to turn it into a naughty, erotic fantasy, she would.

"Alright," she said, lifting her chin. "But you need to do something for me, too."

His eyes glittered dangerously. "What?"

She rose, her body a few scant inches from his. She slipped her thumbs into the waistband of her breeches and pushed them down to her hips. "I can show you how it works better if I have some incentive. Take your pants off, Lachlan, and let me watch you, too." Aislinn was shocked and aroused by the boldness of her own words.

Lachlan stopped breathing for several seconds. She was sure he was going to refuse, but then his nostrils flared and his eyes grew dark, hungry. "Ye first."

She grinned wickedly and slipped the pants down to her ankles. Then she turned and leaned on the bed, giving him a very clear view of her backside and her tiny black thong.

"Sweet Jesu," he whispered, sucking in a breath. She stepped out of her pants and sat on the bed, pushing herself back. Knees up and pressed together, she hid her secrets for a little while longer, looking up at Lachlan expectantly with challenging fire in her green-brown eyes.

"Your turn."

Aislinn had never felt such scorching heat from a man's gaze before, but it was as if he was stroking her with his hands. Slowly, eyes luminous, he stepped out of his boots and kicked them aside. When he lowered his pants, it was Aislinn's turn to gasp. Lachlan's manhood jutted out fiercely proud, intensely aroused. She had to consciously stop herself from whimpering aloud at the sheer size and thickness of it. She had glimpsed it before when she'd peeked under his kilt, but he hadn't been aroused then.

"*Wow*," she breathed. "I mean, *wow*." That part was every bit as large as the rest of him. Incredibly long and thick, a shiver of terror and delight ran up and down the length of her spine.

Aislinn leaned back on one elbow, opening her knees and running the little silvery object along the tiny strip of fabric that hid the most private part of her.

"Stroke yourself," she urged, wondering when she had been possessed by the spirit of a porn star. "Stroke yourself as you watch me."

In front of her, Lachlan gripped himself. His long, thick fingers wrapped around the base of his shaft with a familiarity that had the wetness seeping from her core.

"That's it," she purred, pulling the fabric to one side, exposing the shiny white gold ring there. He licked his lips, as if wanting desperately to run his tongue along it, to pull it lightly between his teeth. At least that's what she pictured him doing in her mind.

"Lovely," he growled.

Aislinn was so filled with need that it only took a few moments to lose herself. But instead of closing her eyes and creating scenes in her mind as she normally would have, she kept them open. Watching Lachlan watch her, seeing him stroke himself with the same rhythm she used on herself – it was beyond erotic. Soon her hips were rocking, curling up to capture that elusive prize dancing just beyond her reach.

Her breathy pants filled the air around them as the pressure mounted. And mounted. Though physically they were not touching, she felt connected to him on a level far deeper than she had anticipated. Holding his gaze, hearing the barely audible hum of her toy and the soft slap of his palm, she climbed higher and higher until finally, she broke.

Aislinn was not a screamer. When she came, it was with the softest of cries, but it was the most powerful climax she had ever experienced. Her legs clamped together, reflexively trying to stem the intensity, even as her body seized in the grips of her pleasure.

Within seconds, Lachlan followed, coating her with his spend from thigh to belly. Eyes still closed in rapture, Aislinn felt the bed dip to one side as he dropped down beside her.

Though he was next to her, they remained physically apart. He made no attempt at post-coital cuddling or spooning, which made sense, since technically, they hadn't really had sex. Aislinn wasn't sure if she was disappointed or relieved.

He was silent for a long time. Aislinn opened her eyes and chanced a look his way. His forearm rested across his eyes; Aislinn had no idea what he was thinking. Wasn't even sure what *she* was thinking, other than the fact that it was the most intimate thing she'd ever experienced.

After the explosive orgasm, Aislinn was feeling less the seductress and more the – well, she really didn't even know how to categorize what she was feeling. Shock at her own actions, definitely. Perhaps a bit of shame, but strangely enough, no regret.

She rose up and gathered a cloth left over from her bath. When she was finished cleaning herself, she rinsed the cloth and padded over to do the same for him.

Lachlan's hand closed around her wrist as he sat up. The look in his eyes was unreadable as he allowed her to clean him, but his expression was clear enough. He looked every bit as confused as she felt.

"I've never done that before," she said quietly, trying to be extra gentle with him.

It was an admission she did not make easily. For as bold as she was, her real-life experience with men was limited. Very few people actually knew that, preferring to judge her particular book by her pierced, badass cover. But had they bothered to look deeper, they would have learned that Aislinn had never found anyone she had wanted to share that kind of intimacy with.

She knew the basics, as well as about a thousand variations. She'd heard about them, read about them, even watched a few videos. Enough to talk the talk and feed the image. But the truth was, she'd never brought herself to climax in front of a man before. Never actually held a man in her hand or felt the steel of a man's erection, sheathed in something that felt like a perfect blend of silk and velvet. Even now, semi-erect, he spilled over her palm.

He searched her eyes, as if they held the

answers he sought.

"I mean, I've done *that*, but never with anyone watching." For some reason, she didn't think he made a habit out of doing that kind of thing either. She felt his embarrassment. In a strange way, it made her feel a little better about her own.

"I'm sorry."

He cupped her chin with his hand and forced her to look at him. "Are ye?"

"Not about this," she said truthfully on an exhale. "That was... unlike anything I've ever felt. Better than I ever could have imagined really." When she felt the color begin to rise in her cheeks at that raw admission – Aislinn did *not* blush – she hastily continued, "I was talking about this morning. I guess women don't normally wear pants around here, huh?"

Lachlan's expression changed at the reminder. Impassivity was replaced with hunger, which was followed quickly by a slight scowl. Aislinn was fascinated by the transformation. For as stoic as he tried to be, his emotions were always right there in his face, if one was looking close enough.

"Nay," he agreed. "They doona." He inhaled and exhaled heavily, running his hand along the back of his neck. "It would make life a lot easier for me, lass, if ye refrained from doing so, at least in front of the men. Ye have free reign in the keep, but mayhap it would be best te steer clear of the areas where they are gathered."

Aislinn considered the big, beautiful man before her, the one with whom she had just shared the most intimate moment of her life thus far. He was turning out to be nothing like she had expected. It should have been difficult to reconcile this humbler side of him with the arrogant, powerful laird, but it wasn't. It was all him, and he didn't insult her by trying to pretend otherwise.

If Lachlan had demanded that she not wear boy's clothing, she would have told him to stick it where the sun didn't shine. But he didn't. He didn't even ask her not to, really, just not to flaunt it.

And that made all the difference in the world.

Chapter 6

Would she respect his wishes? Lachlan wondered the next morning. The Great Hall seemed fuller as men, lads, and even quite a few women lingered over their trenchers longer than usual. Many a curious gaze was trained on the entrance from the far side of the large chamber, the one that led to the private quarters. Those that had the good manners not to stare openly lifted their eyes often to ensure that they would not miss anything.

No doubt word of Aislinn's unconventional entrance yestermorn had piqued their collective interest. Lachlan grunted. He couldn't blame them. No one was more interested than he.

And why shouldn't he be? The woman was a vexing conundrum, appearing out of nowhere, with the mouth and fighting skills of a man but the body and beauty of an angel. Clear-headed and intelligent one moment, spewing nonsense the next. At first glance, she was ferocity personified, but he had witnessed something else, too – flashes of a vulnerability that had his innate male instinct to protect rushing to the surface.

Along with a few other, wholly male instincts.

She was stubborn, too. Despite her English manner of speaking, she had the spirit of a Highlander. The way she lifted that wee chin, pure defiance in her hypnotic eyes - it did something to him, something he could not easily explain.

Lachlan sighed. Even his brothers could not keep their eyes on their trenchers. What the devil had the lass been thinking, donning lad's clothing like that? What if other females suddenly decided they wanted to try it as well? No one would be able to think past the compulsion to rut otherwise, and they were a randy enough bunch as it was. Then again, most females would probably not look as enticing in boy's breeches as Aislinn did.

Most of those in his keep were related to him somehow – brothers, cousins, nephews. He didn't want to have to kill them. Yet the urge to do so had been surprisingly strong when he thought of the way they had looked at Aislinn. He wouldn't allow himself to think about the reasoning behind that, either.

"Finished." Gavin thrust a sheet before him, breaking him from his disturbing thoughts.

Gavin's rendering of Aislinn threatened to take his breath away. Even on parchment, she was a beautiful creature, and Gavin's God-given talent was even more apparent with such a stunning subject.

"She is a fine-looking lass, te be sure," Malcolm breathed over his shoulder. "Have ye been able te learn anything more about her?"

"Nay," Lachlan said, shaking his head. "She keeps her secrets, that one."

"Mayhap ye were no' persuasive enough," Malcolm suggested with an all-too familiar gleam in his eye.

Images of Aislinn naked from the waist down, pleasuring herself while he watched, assaulted him. Of the look on her face when she reached her peak. The thought of anyone else bearing witness to such rapture made the murderous urges surge in his blood again with frightening intensity.

"Ye will no' seduce her," Lachlan commanded, pinning Malcolm with a glare devoid of amusement, one that left no room for misinterpretation. "I forbid it."

Malcolm narrowed his eyes, but nodded. Lachlan was his brother, but he was also his laird.

"If there is anyone who can get the lass te share, 'tis Malcolm," Simon suggested. "Mayhap an escorted tour of the keep will loosen the lass's tongue." The quietest among them, Simon rarely said anything unless he felt it absolutely necessary to do so. For that reason, Lachlan tended to listen whenever he did. He did not particularly like the idea of sending Malcolm to Aislinn, but there was no denying that the libidinous bastard did possess an innate charm that softened a lass's natural defenses.

"Alright," Lachlan reluctantly agreed. There

were a few things he had to see to anyway, and he preferred that Aislinn be kept under a watchful eye. And he *did* trust Malcolm. Randy as the man was, he would not seduce Aislinn if he said he would not. The bigger concern was the possibility of Aislinn falling victim to Malcolm's charms. Then again, beyond a cursory glance, Aislinn hadn't shown the slightest interest in anyone – besides him. A glimmer of hope sparked in his chest.

"Malcolm, give our guest a tour of the keep. Mayhap she will be more of a mind te trust us if we share a bit ourselves, aye? Gavin, take the likeness with ye and see if anyone kens who she is, but be discreet until we ken what we are dealing with. Simon and Conall, go with him."

They nodded their acknowledgement, careful to avert their eyes lest the laird see the triumph that glistened there.

* * *

As Gavin rode off toward the nearest village with Simon and Conall to make and send a few inquiries, Lachlan, Bowen and Aengus revisited the location of the ambush.

"Is this from whence she emerged?" Bowen asked, pointing to a section of trees at the southern end of the small clearing.

"Must have," Lachlan mused, trying to recall his exact positioning before Aislinn's sudden and unexpected appearance. "I was facing this way," he pointed north, "battling McCraes from the front and both sides. I would have seen her if she had been elsewhere."

The men spread out and made their way toward the woods. "What exactly are we looking for?" asked Aengus.

"Anything that might give us a clue as te how she came te be in our midst," Bowen answered. "She says she doesnae ken, that she just opened her eyes and here she was."

Aengus's eyes flicked around the immediate area. "Do ye think she was cudgeled and dumped here against her will?"

"Weel, it would make sense, would it no'? She did have that nasty bump, and it would explain how she came te be here without her knowledge."

"Aye, and it may have addled her brains enough te have her thinking 'tis naught all but a dream," Bowen reasoned.

"But it does no' explain the strange garb, nor the curious blades she carries and uses with such skill."

Or tiny little silver objects that make her come, Lachlan thought to himself as he listened to his brothers thinking out loud.

"Who kens what they do up north?" Bowen muttered. "'Twould no' be the first strange tale ye've heard of those clans."

It was easy enough to see where Aislinn had

lain. The wild grass was still somewhat depressed, a few dark stains still visible from the wound to her head, but otherwise, there was no evidence of any other presence; no footprints, broken foliage, or telltale signs of a horse. Circling outward, they found nothing to indicate the direction from whence she came nor the method of her arrival.

"Bugger," muttered Lachlan.

"There is another possibility," said Bowen slowly.

"Aye? And what might that be?"

"That the lass is spinning tales for some nefarious purpose."

Lachlan was already shaking his head before the last syllable left Bowen's mouth, but Bowen pressed on. "Think upon it, Lachlan. The woman has deadly skill, and is more than a little distracting. Who better te infiltrate a keep overflowing with braw males than a wee female? The McCraes have te ken they have neither the skills nor the strength te breach Dubhain themselves."

Aengus looked thoughtful, almost impressed. "T'would be a brilliant strategy. No' one of us gave a second thought te bringing her inside the walls when she swooned."

Scarily enough, that was true. Had Aislinn wanted to, with her speed and skill and her very effective method of distraction, she could have slit at least a few of their throats before they even realized what was happening. But she hadn't. In fact, ever since they'd taken her inside the gates of Dubhain, she'd been almost docile.

Perhaps her lethal prowess only emerged when she – or someone else – was threatened. That was something Lachlan could understand all too easily, and more than that, it fit seamlessly with every other impression he had already formed about her. The challenging mystery of Aislinn McKenna was coming together quite nicely, in fact.

"She saved my life," he felt compelled to remind them.

"Did she? Mayhap she was part of the plot from the beginning."

Lachlan looked at him with disbelief. Bowen was always playing devil's advocate; it was a talent that had served them well on several occasions, offering possibilities they might not have considered otherwise, yet it chafed now.

"Ye think the men were pawns? Sacrificed for the sole purpose of getting someone inside Dubhain?"

Bowen shrugged. "'Twould not be the first betrayal of its kind, and Dubhain is a fine enough prize te risk a few sacrifices."

She would not betray me, Lachlan thought fiercely, the truth of it ringing through him with surprising clarity, even though he could summon no rational basis for it.

"I admit, t'would be quite a boon, but it does no' feel right, somehow," Aengus said, scratching at his neck.

Lachlan shot him a grateful look. Where Bowen had the ability to think beyond a situation, Aengus was often the voice of logic. If he didn't think Aislinn meant them harm, it would go a long way in convincing the others.

"The McCrae are just no' that cunning; based on our previous experiences with them, they are far more likely te use brawn over brain. And I can no' say why, exactly, but I doona believe the lass is spinning tales. I get the feeling she is every bit as vexed as we are. Did ye see the way she looks around her, as if she has never seen the likes of a keep in her life?"

"Then how do ye explain it, Aengus? Do ye think that Fate and Fae plucked the wee lass from wherever she was and placed her at our doorstep?"

Aengus frowned, but Lachlan remained quiet. That is *exactly* what he was beginning to think.

* * *

Malcolm hid a grin as Aislinn grimaced and shifted yet again, clearly unused to maneuvering amidst such copious amounts of fabric. The lass was as buggered as a kitten in a sack. Of the tasks appointed to them this morn, he definitely had the most enviable. The fact that it irked his staid and implacable older brother was an added bonus.

It was something he thought he might never

see. Lachlan was a good man and a good laird. He cared for his people, was objective and fair, and asked none to perform a duty he would not have (or had not) done himself. He was much loved and respected, and placed the needs of those around him above his own.

But where Aislinn was concerned, Lachlan was different. Rather than placing her under the care of another as would have been prudent, Lachlan had appointed himself the lass's keeper. He was fiercely possessive of her as well, warning off any who sought to engage the lass in any way.

Malcolm was not the only one who noticed. The rest of his brothers agreed that Lachlan might not be thinking too clearly where their unexpected guest was concerned, and felt a collective need to intervene. The laird's uncharacteristic behavior was the primary reason why they had secretly conspired to suggest this little escorted tour.

Lachlan would no doubt figure it out eventually, but in this instance, they all believed that it was better to ask forgiveness than permission. Malcolm had no doubt he would be able to make Lachlan see the merits of their scheming after the fact.

In reality, Malcolm's purpose was two-fold – to discover a little more about Aislinn by observing her reactions to various things while engaging her in conversation, and to keep her from causing a full-scale riot among the males. Already yestermorn's tale of Aislinn's appearance in the Great Hall was fast becoming legend, despite the fact that the room had only been half-full at the time.

Except there *had* been a suspicious number of mischievous lads loitering about, it had seemed. His own son Rory had looked especially gleeful, in fact.

* * *

"Ye look quite fetching, lass."

"Thanks," Aislinn said doubtfully, tugging at the bodice. "I think. That is a compliment, isn't it? Or is it a polite way of telling me I look utterly ridiculous?" Because that's exactly how she felt.

"Nay," Malcolm laughed. "Ye do look lovely. A vision, in fact."

Aislinn blushed slightly and turned away, unused to such compliments. The way Malcolm spoke, she could almost believe he meant it. He could teach Johnny Depp a thing or two about smooth.

"So, you're my babysitter, I take it?"

"Babysitter?" he frowned, unfamiliar with the term.

"You get to keep an eye on me, make sure I don't cause any trouble until you decide what to do with me."

His eyes widened ever so slightly, the only indication that she had hit the nail right on the head. It was all the confirmation she needed.

"I prefer te think of myself as the mon fortunate enough te have the enviable task of showing you around whilst enjoying the pleasure of your company."

Aislinn grinned at that. "My, my. Such charm. No wonder there are so many auburn-haired little boys with flashing green eyes around here."

Malcolm roared with laughter. "Truly, ye are a delight, Lady Aislinn. Come," he said offering his arm, "and I will give ye the grand tour."

After hesitating for a few moments, she finally threaded her hand through the crook of Malcolm's elbow, the same way she had seen other women doing when escorted around the keep. Like Lachlan, Malcolm was tall and broad, and she felt very small beside him as they wound their way through the stone-walled corridors.

For a dream it was very realistic. Aislinn was impressed with her own creativity and attention to detail. The hand-woven tapestries that hung on the walls were intricately done, each one crafted in the clan's color scheme and depicting a varied array of scenes, from epic battles to everyday life in the Highlands.

The walls were all made out of stone, as she might have expected, but she didn't think she would have imagined the hand-blown oil lamps in expertly-worked metal sconces, or the way certain veins in the stone reflected the flames. Rough-fibered runners softened the echo of their footsteps, while fresh rushes and herbs scattered about kept the halls and rooms smelling clean and fresh.

After touring the Great Hall, the common areas, and the kitchens, Malcolm led her outside and into the bailey, where some of the lads were practicing their swordplay. Rory was there, and made quite a show of bowing deeply to Aislinn, then grinning and giving her a wink.

"Ye seem te have made quite an impression on the lads, Lady Aislinn," Malcolm observed as they continued on toward the stables.

"They're good kids," Aislinn answered. "It's nice that you take responsibility for them like you do."

"The Brodie take care of their own."

"So I've heard," she murmured, remembering Rory using those same words. Perhaps it was a Brodie credo or something. "Not all are as fortunate." She paused. "Can I ask you something, Malcolm?"

"Aye, o' course."

"Do you take the little girls, too?"

Malcolm seemed surprised by the question. "Lasses?"

"Yes, the lasses. I have seen lots of little boys running around the keep but no little girls. What happens when one of them is born out of wedlock? Who cares for them?"

Malcolm looked down into Aislinn's eyes, and saw the pain there before she could fully hide it behind a mask of righteous indignation. "I doona believe we have ever had that issue," he said honestly. "'Tis a blessing of the Brodie bloodline to bear sons, nay so much daughters."

"So what are the daughters, then? Curses? Mistakes?"

"Nay," Malcolm said, taken aback by the vehemence in her tone. "'Twould truly be a gift of God to be blessed with a wee angel. It just has no' happened."

Apparently Aislinn was unconvinced, because she pulled away and started walking in front of him. Malcolm took two long strides before reaching for her arm and turning her to face him. "But if it does, ye can rest assured a Brodie lass would be treated like a right princess, and be the best protected lass in all o' the Isles."

Aislinn's features softened a little, then hardened as she looked pointedly at where his hand now gripped her upper arm. Malcolm released her, but his hopes that the lass would be sharing anything with him that day fell by the wayside.

Chapter 7

Later that eve, Lachlan stood just inside the doorway, holding his breath. Aislinn was contorting her body in alluring ways, her most womanly parts barely concealed with minimal scraps of fabric. She moved slowly, gracefully. Eyes closed, she hummed softly beneath her breath as her body fluidly transitioned from one pose to the next. It was both beautiful and hypnotic, requiring great strength and control. Lachlan was immediately transfixed by the firm, solid tone of her flesh, so unlike the softer, rounder women he was used to.

Malcolm had told him what had transpired earlier, admitting to the brothers' premeditated motives as well as his failure to extract much in the way of useful information. At first, Lachlan had been annoyed by their sly manipulation, but he understood it. Where Aislinn was concerned, he *was* acting out of character. Had any one of them been in the same situation, he would not have thought twice about doing likewise.

And Malcolm's time with Aislinn had not been completely uninformative. Aislinn's questions about the lack of female children and her subsequent reaction were quite revealing, in fact. It added a few more pieces to the intriguing puzzle that was Aislinn. A puzzle that he found himself increasingly interested in solving.

Aislinn didn't seem aware of his presence, so he was surprised when she greeted him.

"Hi, Lachlan," she said without opening her eyes. "I'll be finished in a minute."

Glad for the opportunity to observe for a little longer, Lachlan leaned his big frame against the wall and answered, "Take yer time." Her body continued to move, her slightly bronzed skin golden in the flickering candle light, brief flashes of sparkle glinting as the flames were captured by the ring in her navel.

"What was that ye were doing?" Lachlan asked as Aislinn finished and wiped the slight sheen of perspiration from her brow.

"A combination of yoga and pilates," she answered. When he looked at her questioningly, she explained, "It's a way to calm the mind and the body, to center yourself."

He nodded in comprehension. "I spar with my brothers when things begin te weigh too heavily. Hitting them always makes me feel better."

"That works too," she laughed. "And now that you mention it, I could use a good workout. I'm not used to sitting around all day. Yoga helped some, but I'm still feeling a little jacked-up. What do you say? Are you up for it?"

It took a few moments for Lachlan to translate her words into something he could understand. When he did, his eyes opened wide. "Ye wish te spar with me?"

"Yeah. You look like you're a bit on the edge, too."

He was, but probably not for the reasons she thought. He felt strung as tightly as a newly-hewn bow. He could not dispel the images of her pleasuring herself from his mind, nor shake off the visceral pleasure of spilling on her golden skin. He wanted *more*.

"Nay," he said, shaking his head. He had much better ways to expend his pent-up energy. And while they all included close physical contact, none of them involved him hurting her. Given his much greater size and strength, even the slightest miscalculation could cause her serious harm.

"Why not?"

Lachlan crossed his massive arms over his chest and spoke with all the authority of a man used to being in charge. "*Ye are a lass.* And a wee lass at that. Ye would be better off tussling with the lads. They are more your size."

* * *

Aislinn narrowed her eyes, trying not to be too distracted by the sensual rippling and bunching of muscles beneath his skin. The cocky bastard was probably doing it on purpose.

"Maybe I'm not some great hulking brute, but I *am* the girl who saved your ass and is seriously considering kicking it now just for the sheer fun of it."

He stood a little taller, his voice growing softer and all that much more dangerous because of it. "Ye are threatening me?"

There was no way she was going to win in a direct face-off against this guy, she decided. Playing a little dirty was not totally out of the question. When the odds were stacked against you, you had to grab every advantage, right?

"Hey, I understand if you're not up for it. I mean, you are getting up there in age. You're like what, forty?" she taunted, knowing he wasn't anywhere near that, as well as the fact that he was in peak physical condition. Even among the elite Rangers she'd never seen someone quite so drool-worthy, and that was saying something.

If he was thinking with his brain instead of his manly pride he would have realized that, but Aislinn was betting on his testosterone. Any man that size would have to have that particular hormone in spades.

"Maybe I should ask Gavin. I bet *he'd* spar with me. He's almost as big as you, and way younger."

It had been a calculated gamble, but Aislinn

knew it had paid off by the way Lachlan narrowed his eyes. She couldn't have picked a name that would have affected him more. Gavin was the youngest of the brothers, around twenty or so, and nearly perfect of face and form. Malcolm had even joked earlier that Gavin alone had the ability to charm a nun from her vows with naught but a smile from his bonnie face.

But while Gavin was nice to look at, he didn't set her heart to racing like Lachlan did. Fortunately for her, Lachlan didn't know that.

"Fine," he huffed. "Have it yer way. But doona cry when this *old mon* puts ye over his knee and spanks yer insolent arse."

* * *

Soon after, they found themselves out in the glen beneath the moonlight, circling each other warily. By mutual agreement they did not use real weapons; Lachlan managed to pick up a few wooden swords like the ones the lads used to practice in the courtyard.

He had known she was quick, but he hadn't realized just how fast she really was. Now that she had had a chance to rest and heal, she moved like lightning, in one place one moment and somewhere else the next, flipping and twisting in the air but always landing on her feet. She came at him from all sides, scoring an impressive array of hits with her tiny bare feet, though each one was little more than a tap. What was even more amazing to him was that she was deliberately pulling her strikes, as if *she* was afraid of hurting *him*.

Once he got over his initial shock, he realized that he had no hopes of catching her; she was simply too small and too fast. His best strategy was to conserve his energy, keep himself loosely planted and let her come to him in the hope that she would tire and begin to make some mistakes.

She seemed to be enjoying herself immensely. Strangely enough, he was too. He loved watching her move. She was lithe and beautiful; catching her would be a prize indeed. Never would he have believed that sparring with a woman could be quite so invigorating. It helped, of course, that Aislinn was no ordinary female. With each passing moment his respect – and desire - for her grew.

"Come on, old man," she teased as she leaped, spun in the air, and landed yet another blow against the back of his shoulder, only to land in a crouch just out of arm's reach. "I promise I won't hurt you. Much."

Lachlan growled at her, his heart beating in anticipation. The few heavy-handed smacks he managed to land on her backside only seemed to energize her. He turned with her, following her movements as she danced all around him. After a while, he began to detect a pattern. Anticipating her next move as she came around him, his hand shot out and grabbed at her ankle, catching her mid-kick.

Aislinn adjusted in a heartbeat, twisting in his hand. When Lachlan saw her other leg coming up to hit him squarely in the chest, he countered the move and swung his other hand in a horizontal arc, deflecting the blow. With his great shove and the momentum from her intended kick, she went down hard several feet away.

When she didn't get right back up and come after him, fear gripped him. "Aislinn?"

"What?!?" She bit out the answer through gritted teeth.

"Are ye hurt, lass?"

"I'm fine. Just give me a minute."

Stubborn female. In two strides he was beside her. She was still on the ground, her back to him, breathing heavily.

"Where does it hurt, lass?" he asked, crouching down.

"Gotcha." Before he could process what was happening, she twisted, wrapped both legs around his head and twisted again, using leverage and the element of surprise to pull him off balance and bring him down to his knees. In a fluid move, she swung onto his back as if he was a horse. Then with a wicked laugh, she turned around spanked *him*.

It was more than he could take.

More than any man could be expected to take.

Lachlan Brodie, the staid and respected laird of Dubhain, snapped.

Seconds later, Aislinn was beneath him, gasping for breath as he pressed his substantial weight down upon her.

"Is that how ye want te play it then, lass?" he said, his voice soft, controlled. "Ye resort te trickery? Play upon a mon's honor?"

Holding her in place, he tugged down her leggings as she writhed beneath him. With one swift and easy move, he rolled off of her and pulled her over his lap. She struggled and wiggled, torturing him, but she was no match for a riled Brodie. One heavy hand landed on her backside and she howled. His palm smoothed over the soft, quickly reddening flesh. Then he did it again. And again.

Adrenalin coursed through his veins, his senses sharp and alert. The echoes of her howls in his ears, the sight of her arse, blossoming such a pretty red beneath his hand, had the blood boiling in his cock. He flipped her over, petting her with a softer hand, fascinated by her bare sex.

"So smooth. So soft." It was a hoarse whisper as his hands stroked her with wonder.

She stopped struggling.

Her scent hit him then, heady and potent, and Lachlan could no longer restrain himself. Pushing her back onto the ground, he kneeled between her legs, spreading them wider so he could look down at her bare, glistening sex. She wrapped her legs around his neck again, but this time, it was not an attempt to best him or to flee. This time it was an urgent demand. She fisted her hands in his hair, raising her hips toward him as she pulled at his head.

He'd never had a woman so eager for his intimate kiss. Alas, it was not something a proper lass would allow. The one and only time he had attempted such a bold act, he was rebuffed and treated with disgust. But this was no proper lass. This was Aislinn. She was a warrior, and an angel. And she *wanted* this. Almost as much as he did.

Lachlan lowered his head and buried his face in her sex. Perhaps she would not notice his lack of skill if he was ardent enough.

"Wait!" He heard the harsh plea and his heart fell until she uttered her next words. "I want to taste you too…"

Using her powerful legs, she guided him onto his back. Secure in the knowledge that she would not deny him, he allowed her to lead. She turned and stretched, pushing at his trews, urging him to lift his hips. Unable to do anything but obey, he did. In one moment, he felt the cool night air upon his heated flesh. In the next, she was straddling his face with her sex and scalding his manhood with her hot little mouth.

He was beyond thought; the woman was straight out of his darkest and most sinful fantasies, yet he could find nothing but pure bliss in her touch.

To pleasure and be pleasured in this way was beyond his wildest dreams. He was intoxicated by the taste and scent of her, as aware of her desperate desire as he was of his own. His tongue danced with the dangling ring before dipping deep into her honeyed center, insane with hunger for more.

She rode his face with wild abandon; he gripped her hips, holding her to him while she pulled and stroked his cock. The weight of her splayed across his stomach, her heat soaking into him, warming him down to his very soul. Her hard nipples and the rings adorning them stroked against the skin of his abdomen as she sucked hard at him, pumping him with one hand while she squeezed his testicles with the other. Silken tresses teased his inner thighs, an erotic tickle that had his balls aching for release.

There was nothing he could do to stop the seed from rising in his shaft. As much as he wanted to spill into that wicked mouth, he had to warn her. If he didn't, she might never agree to do this again, and that was simply unacceptable. He would not willingly give this up for a few brief moments of selfish pleasure. With great effort, he forced the words out against her sex.

"Aislinn, angel, I'm goin' te … so hard!"

Instead of pulling away, however, she redoubled her efforts. She gripped him harder, stroked him faster. She groaned, the vibrations rippling down his shaft even as she rode him more frantically, a fresh wave of sweet cream spilling across his tongue. Could it be that the thought of him finding release actually aroused her?

All doubts were erased when the first pulse ripped through him. She moaned and took him so deep he could actually feel the constriction of her throat muscles around him as she swallowed. It was mimicked by the clenching of her sheath as her powerful thighs squeezed around his head. The strength of her orgasm had her seizing and shuddering, and still, he came.

When she had wrung every last drop of spend from him, she licked him like a contented cat. Her body, limp and languid, draped over him. She offered no resistance when he reached down and turned her around, drawing her up onto his chest. Her head burrowed into his neck.

There were no words. When his heart slowed to a normal rhythm and he was able to breathe freely again, he simply wrapped his arms around her and held her until she stopped trembling. Then he carried her back to the keep.

He didn't bother taking her to the guest room.

Hands shaking and heart pounding, he dared not ask permission lest she deny him. Aislinn's arms were wrapped around his neck, her soft body held tightly to his chest.

"You must be very strong to carry me like this," she murmured, her voice thick and sensual.

A beam of silvery moonlight played across her features. A glance down revealed that her eyes were closed, her expression one of satisfaction and serenity. His grip unconsciously tightened, afraid of letting her go.

"Ye are wee," he breathed huskily. "'Tis no great feat." She was like warm silk in his arms; he carried her easily.

"Big enough to take you on," she murmured, sending little puffs of breath across his skin.

"Aye," he agreed. She was a worthy partner indeed. Beautiful and intelligent, a skilled warrioress with a passion rivaling his own.

He laid her gently upon his bed, as gently as a man like him could. When she didn't release him, but instead pulled him down onto her, he wanted to shout out in thanks and triumph.

"Make love to me, Lachlan," she purred, her hand skimming between them, searching for and finding his manhood. Though only minutes earlier he had spent himself, her touch had him hard and aching again. His fingers dipped down into her sex, finding her swollen and slick. No woman had ever been so ready for him.

"Aye," he answered. As if he was capable of denying her.

"Be gentle at first, okay?" she asked, so quietly he barely heard it over the heated blood rushing through his body. Yet she might have screamed it in his ear for the effect it had. His fingers dipped inside her again, searching.

And finding.

"Aislinn," he breathed, awestruck by the proof

that this intensely passionate, sexual creature was unbreached.

"It's okay, Lachlan," she encouraged softly, her hands making petty strokes along his shoulders, his back. Though he had come within a hair's breadth of viciously ripping through her maidenhead, *she* was soothing *him*.

"Ye are an innocent," he said roughly.

To his surprise, she laughed softly. "I don't think anyone's ever called me that before. Hellion, demon spawn, -"

Lachlan stopped her painful words with a brush of his lips over hers. "Ye are nothing less than an angel te me, Aislinn. An angel out of my wildest dreams."

No one had ever said kinder words to her. Tears welled in her eyes. "Make love to me, Lachlan," she repeated. "*Please.*"

The honorable part of him knew that he should give her pleasure without stealing her innocence. That he should hold her and stroke her until she was so satisfied that penetration didn't matter. But another part of him could not forego this chance to claim her, to be the first and only man to ever receive this gift from her. Before he could think on it too much, before his honorable conscience could reason with his primal male, he plunged deep and true, capturing her soft cries with his mouth.

Chapter 8

"Tell me about these," he said quietly, flicking one of her nipple rings lightly with his fingers. She moaned softly, snuggling closer against him. After his breaching, he spent the next several hours making slow, passionate love to her. He made certain that her first (and second, third, and fourth) times were memorable and wrought as much pleasure as humanly possible.

"What do you want to know?" she murmured sleepily. He loved the sated, sensual tone of her voice.

"What is their purpose?"

"Purpose?" she echoed, drawing herself up on one elbow as she considered his question. "Pride, I guess. At least at first. The guys in my unit dared me to."

He tensed, the thought of Aislinn being around other males creating an unpleasant, clawing sensation deep in his chest. She must have felt it, because a moment later she was stroking him there, calming him almost instantly.

"Relax. It wasn't like that. We were all soldiers, nothing more. They were damn good men, and we made one hell of a team. After a particularly bad mission, we went out and got drunk. It turned into a classic case of one-upmanship – who could handle more pain. For every piercing I got, they each had to get one too."

Lachlan winced at that, instinctively squeezing his legs together, making Aislinn chuckle. "Yeah, that's what they thought, too. It only hurts for a little bit, though. Then it's sensitive as hell."

To prove her point, she leaned over his chest and lightly bit his nipple. Lachlan sucked in a breath as she gave him a couple of soothing licks and blew cold air over the tips. "See? They say it's even more erotic *down there.* At least it is for me."

Aislinn draped her thigh over his. "I know whatever you were doing down there felt absolutely *amazing*."

Lachlan cupped her behind possessively and responded with a wholly masculine grunt that reflected both pleasure and smug satisfaction.

"And yer markings?" he asked, tracing the Celtic knots with the pads of his fingers.

"They're more complicated," she said. "Those, I did for no one but me. I can't even tell you why, exactly. Just that I was stationed in the U.K. and had some time to kill. I walked into an ink shop and was looking through some designs, and these – I don't know, this is going to sound really weird – they *meant* something to me. After I got them, I didn't feel quite so alone. For some reason, they make me feel like I am connected with something bigger than myself, if that makes any sense."

"Aye, it does," he said, tucking her close. "Do ye not ken what they mean?"

"Not with any degree of accuracy, no."

"Then I will tell ye," he said. "The symbols ye chose are both ancient and powerful. The series of knots here are as complex as any as I have ever seen. The knot itself is a symbol of continuity – no beginning and no end. 'Tis a symbol of life, of nature, and of love."

"Now, the fact that ye have not one but several variations is significant, for the shape further defines the meaning. This one here – ye see how it is an oval? That represents life and the eternal cycle of birth, death, and rebirth. Triangular knots – like these – represent unity with the world around us. Some believe it te be earth, sky and sea, but others say it is specific te the Holy Trinity – Father, Son, and Holy Ghost. And the square ones – they are symbols of love. The unbroken lines symbolize love and faithfulness."

"They make ye feel a part of the world around ye, Aislinn, because ye are. Yer heart and soul ken it, even if yer head does no'."

She looked at him with something like awe. "How do you know all this?"

"Because," he smiled, "'tis *my* heritage ye are wearing." He patted her softly on the behind. "Come," he said, easing out of bed. "There is something I've been wanting te show ye."

Dressed in nothing but Lachlan's shirt – which extended well past her knees – Lachlan held her hand and led her through the quiet, deserted corridors of his home. Neither of them spoke, walking along on silent feet until Lachlan finally stopped before a large oak door. Whatever lay beyond had not been part of Malcolm's tour; Aislinn was certain she would have remembered this door, with its beautiful, intricate carvings.

With a quick kiss, Lachlan fished out a key and fitted it into the lock. The huge door swung open easily and quietly upon well-oiled hinges.

Aislinn sucked in a breath as Lachlan made his way around the room lighting the torch lamps secured in wrought sconces upon the wall.

"This is the portrait hall of the Brodie clan," he told her.

Aislinn looked around in awe, studying each painted portrait, all hung in regal frames around the room. Of big, handsome men with familiar auburn hair and luminous green eyes. Of women and children around them. Lachlan moved with her, watching her carefully.

"This is you," she breathed, bringing her hands up to a family portrait. Lachlan looked around Rory's age or so, but even then there was no mistaking the familiar tilt of his jaw or the eyes that seemed to see right down into her soul. He stood proudly between what must have been his parents, surrounded by five devilish looking boys at various ages.

"Aye," he said. "'My father consigned a new portrait every time our family expanded. That is the last one."

"But there are only six of you," she said, counting. "That's Malcolm, that's Conall. Simon. Aengus. Bowen. Wait – where's Gavin?"

"There is no family portrait containing Gavin," he said quietly, his voice tinged with sadness. "Our mother died in childbirth, and my Da could no' bear te have one done without her."

"Oh, Lachlan. I'm so very sorry," Aislinn said, laying her hand upon his forearm.

"'Twas a long time ago," he said, though some pain, he realized, never completely went away. "'Tis both a mon's finest blessing and his biggest curse te get his wife with child. Many of our women die upon the birthing bed. But my mother had already given my Da six strapping, hale lads without issue. No one expected…"

He was quiet for a long time. Aislinn slid her arms around him, holding him, offering the only comfort she could. Lachlan was awed by the warmth that spread through him. He could actually feel the ragged edges of his soul beginning to knit together.

"My Da, he dinnae last much longer. Within half a year, he was gone, too. 'Twas a rare bond they shared, heart and soul. My Da simply could no' go on without her. She was everything te him."

"She was a beautiful woman."

"Aye, she was, in heart as well as her bonnie face. She was a wee thing, like ye, but every bit as strong as a mon on the inside. A true Brodie, she was," he said proudly. He ran a few silken tendrils of her hair through his fingers. "I think she would have liked ye, Aislinn."

He glanced down at her when he heard her soft intake of breath, but she turned her head away. Needing to see the look in her eyes, he cupped her chin between his thumb and forefinger, applying gentle pressure until she met his gaze. He was stunned when he saw them glistening with unshed tears.

"Lass?" he questioned softly.

She blinked rapidly. "It's just… well, I'm not exactly the type of girl most guys would bring home to meet Mom, you know?"

There was that hint of vulnerability again, the one that made him want to gather her up in his arms and ensure that nothing ever put tears in those beguiling eyes again. But as he leaned over to do just that, Aislinn took a step back, crossing her arms over her chest and clearing her throat. "So, how old were you when she passed?"

Surprisingly, her withdrawal stung. Had she not just felt compelled to comfort him when she sensed his sorrow? Why was he not permitted to do the same for her?

Feeling rather cheated, he refrained from crushing her to his chest. Instead, he took her hand in his and returned his gaze to the portrait, vowing to tear down those walls she had built around herself. She *would* come to trust him.

"Eleven summers and half."

"Wait – does that mean you became the laird of Dubhain at the age of *twelve*?"

"I had uncles te help me, but aye."

"You were so young."

"As the eldest son, 'twas my great honor and duty," he said simply, without resentment or anger or any of the other things he might have added.

"And I thought I'd had to grow up fast," she muttered under her breath.

"Tell me," he coaxed.

She opened her mouth, then shook her head. "Another time, maybe. I think I'd just like to go back to bed now."

Lachlan nodded, hiding his disappointment. As much as he wanted answers, the lass needed her rest. He locked up the hall and escorted her back toward the private chambers. When she made to turn into the guest chamber, he tightened his grip on her hand and led her to his.

Thankfully, she did not protest.

* * *

"What did ye find?" Lachlan asked, glancing

out the window into the southeast courtyard where Aislinn was sparring with Rory and several of the other lads. She was wearing breeches, but as a compromise, she had agreed to bind her torso and wear a tunic that extended beyond the curves of her shapely behind. As an added concession, she braided her hair and tucked it beneath the tunic. There was still no mistaking her as anything but a female, but she drew much less attention this way.

It was Conall who answered first. "Several people who knew the missing lass said they share similarities in terms of features."

"But?" Lachlan prompted, hearing the word not spoken.

"But they also said that she was as meek and quiet as a newborn kitten."

"That does no' sound like our Aislinn," Malcolm said. The possessive word flowed easily from his lips, earning a dark scowl from Lachlan. As far as he was concerned, Aislinn was his, but there was no denying that all of his brothers had become fond of her, as had many of the castle staff, and the younglings.

As if on cue, her musical laughter wafted through the window, affectionate taunts at the young lads who could not get close enough to land a single strike. One yelped as she landed a blow to his backside with the flat side of the wooden sword, but Lachlan knew the only thing even slightly stung was the lad's pride. As deadly as she was, he also knew she would never harm an innocent, especially not a child.

Gavin's face grew dark. "Many believe the lass planned her own disappearance. 'Twas rumored that her Da beat her regularly. A few even suggested that we would be doing the lass a favor if we stopped asking questions and let sleeping dogs lie."

"What did they say her name was, this missing lass?"

"Isobeille," Gavin said gravely. "Isobeille *Aislinn McKenna.*"

* * *

"Isobeille." Lachlan murmured the name quietly to see if there was any reaction. There was.

Aislinn looked up at him with pure fire in her eyes as her nails curled into his flesh like tiny claws. "Did you forget who was sharing your bed, Laird Brodie?"

He chuckled as the relief spread through him, and he was now forced to think quickly to soothe his ruffled wee wildcat.

"Are ye sure yer name is Aislinn?" he teased. "Because ye look like an Isobeille te me."

"Yeah, well, maybe you don't look like a Lachlan to me," she sniffed indignantly.

"Oh?" he asked, loving the playful banter that came so easily with her. He had bedded many women, but could not recall a single instance where he had laughed with one in bed, or even talked, for that matter. He found he liked doing both with Aislinn.

"And what name comes te mind when ye look at me?" He puffed out his chest and flexed his great muscles in a show of male prowess.

She considered him only briefly as her mind searched for the most non-threatening name she could think of. "Mortimer."

He bellowed out a laugh, gathering her into his arms and tickling her until she squealed. "Wench."

"Seriously, do you really like the name Isobeille?" Aislinn asked when she was able to breathe again. She snuggled against him, stroking her fingers along his chest. It was something she did often, this gentle petting, though she seemed unaware that she was doing so.

"Aye, 'tis a fine name. Not quite as fine as Aislinn, though," he added with a gentle kiss to the top of her head.

"Well, it's just kind of weird."

"What is?"

"That you thought of that name in particular."

"Why?" he asked, starting to feel a twinge of unease.

"Because that's my middle name. Aislinn *Isobeille* McKenna."

"Is it now?" The words were spoken softly. Lachlan was afraid to speak any louder for fear his voice would betray him. He was not an overly superstitious man by nature, or one to look hard for connections and meanings unseen, but this was a coincidence even he was wary of dismissing easily. That two women would both have the same surname was not the issue – McKenna was quite a common clan name. But that one – Isobeille Aislinn – went missing right around the same time another – Aislinn Isobeille – arrived seemingly out of nowhere … *that* gave him definite pause.

"Yes. Isobeille was my mother's name, a family name that supposedly goes way back. I was named for both her and my dad's mom – her name was Aislinn, I'm told."

"Was, ye say? Yer mother passed?"

She sighed and melted into his chest. "Yes. So did my father. And my brother. And my sister. All at the same time."

His heart twisted in his chest. He wrapped his arms around her and held her tightly against him, as if he could somehow draw some of the pain away from her. It also ensured that she would not slip away from him so easily this time. "How did it happen?"

"Car accident," she said quietly. "My mother was pregnant with me at the time. They kept her on life-support till I was born, but then they disconnected her and she died." She spoke the words simply, with little emotion, as if she was talking about someone else's tragedy instead of her own.

Lachlan felt the horror, even if some of her words were unknown to him. This was not the pain of a woman spinning tales. This was all too real. "What were their names?"

"My mother was Isobeille, as I said. My father was Jack. My brother, Sean. My sister, Maggie. I don't know much about them, except that Maggie was four and Sean was two when it happened."

Lachlan stroked her hair, not knowing what else to do. "Sometimes I wish I'd died, too," she confessed, her voice barely more than a whisper in the dark.

"I am glad ye dinnae, my wee angel. I am verra glad ye dinnae."

Chapter 9

"'Tis no' her," Lachlan said emphatically, bringing his fist down on the table. "Aislinn is no' Isobeille." He wished he had never gone along with Bowen's suggestion to speak the name aloud when her guard was down to gauge her response. He wished even more he had not told them that Isobeille was Aislinn's middle name.

"Mayhap no', but ye have te at least consider the possibility that 'tis more than mere coincidence."

"I did consider it, and that is all that it is. Aislinn's parents *died*."

"So she says."

Bowen didn't even see Lachlan move. "Accuse her of spinning tales again and I will no' hesitate te make sure ye doona talk for a month," Lachlan said through clenched teeth, his hand around his younger brother's throat as he pinned him up against the wall.

"No one is accusing her of lying, Lachlan. She believes what she is saying, we are all in accord on that," Conall said in a logical, even tone.

Lachlan released his brother, leaving him

drawing breath in great gulps. "So ye are saying she is daft?" he seethed, growing larger. "That does no' seem any less insulting."

"Not daft. Jesu, Lachlan, will ye listen te yerself? We only want te help the lass."

"We *are* helping her. 'Tis no place safer for her than Dubhain. I fail te see how offering her up te the mon who supposedly beat her will serve her any better."

"We are no' talking about her Da, Lachlan," said Malcolm quietly. "Someone else has answered the inquiries as weel."

"Who?"

Aengus blew out a breath. "Her betrothed."

Lachlan went completely still. "Excuse me? I doona think I heard ye correctly."

"A mon claiming te be Isobeille McKenna's betrothed has sent word that he would like te see the lass, see for himself if she is his beloved."

"Nay." Lachlan shook his head. It was not possible. If Aislinn was promised to another, he would *know*. No woman could make love with him the way she did and belong to another. Something niggled at the back of his mind, but he cast it aside. "Aislinn is *no'* betrothed."

"But Lachlan - "

"I said, *nay*. Aislinn is no' Isobeille. Let the mon search elsewhere."

"What man?" Aislinn asked, walking into the Great Hall, looking fresh and as beautiful as ever.

Her cheeks were still somewhat flushed from Lachlan's earlier impulsive yet thorough lovemaking.

Lachlan shot a lethal glare at his brother. Aislinn came up to him and laid her hand on his arm, the pads of her fingers making tiny movements along his skin. It had an immediate calming effect.

"She deserves te ken, Lachlan."

He loved his brethren, but so help him they did not know when to keep their mouths shut. Lachlan blew out a breath and looked down into Aislinn's upturned face. One look at the question in her eyes and he knew she expected him to answer.

"A young woman disappeared from one of the Northern clans a few weeks before you came to Dubhain. Her name is Isobeille McKenna, and 'tis said ye favor her likeness."

"And you think I might be her?" Aislinn guessed, reminding Lachlan that she was clever as well as beautiful and deadly. Her eyes narrowed, and the small petting strokes ceased. "That's why you called me Isobeille. To see how I would react to the name."

"Aye," he admitted. "But I doona think ye are her," he was quick to add. Thankfully, her features softened slightly.

"Good, because I'm not." She turned to the others. "Look, I may not know how I came to be on your land, but I *do* know who I am. And dream or not, I have a lifetime of memories that I can guarantee you are mine and mine alone, and none of them could possibly belong to this missing woman."

"The mind is capable of many things," Conall suggested, ignoring Lachlan's repeated warning glares over Aislinn's head. "It is said that Isobeille had a less than ideal life."

"Then that makes two of us. And I get what you're saying, I really do. But believe me when I tell you that if I was so traumatized as to create my own alternate reality, I would not have picked the life I remember. I would love to not have those memories."

Conall did not seem convinced, but he did not press her further.

"Yer life," Lachlan said later that night when Aislinn was properly spent from his ardent lovemaking. "Was it that bad?"

"Yes," she whispered, burrowing deeper into his neck, but she said nothing more.

* * *

"Lachlan, did ye hear me?" Aengus's voice, as well as his swift fist to Lachlan's upper arm, finally got his attention. "What?"

"Jesu, where are ye?" Aengus said, shaking his head. "'Tis no' like ye te be so wool-headed, Lachlan."

"I have much te think upon," Lachlan replied vaguely. For the past three nights he had had

Aislinn in his bed. Three nights of incredible passion. Three nights of deep, contented sleep. Three mornings of waking up to Aislinn loving him with her hands, her mouth, her body. The time in between was a constant replay of images and a desire to be with her again. It was playing havoc with his sensibilities.

"Aye, I guess ye do at that. I said, Simon and Bowen are heading into town. They wish te take Aislinn with them."

Lachlan silenced the immediate and vehement denial that rose in his throat. He had appointments at the keep and would be unable to leave. He couldn't for the life of him remember what those appointments were – it seemed his thoughts lately were almost exclusively of one particular lass - but some vague notion suggested they were important.

He could simply forbid her to go. The thought of Aislinn being that far away from him did not sit well. She was adjusting rather well to life around the keep, but the village? There were a lot of hale young males there whose eye would undoubtedly be drawn her way. Aislinn had a way of standing out.

"Do ye think that wise?"

"She has promised te wear proper attire," Aengus grinned. "No more breeches or lad's shirts. And te – as she put it – *zip her lips*, which we assume means te keep quiet. In truth, she seems quite excited about the idea."

A soft growl emanated from the back of

Lachlan's throat. *He* wanted to be the one to accompany her into the village and show Aislinn around. He wanted to see her face as she discovered things. He loved the way everything seemed new to her. It was like experiencing everything anew through her eyes. Aislinn had a very unique way of looking at things, a way of challenging his mind that was every bit as enticing as the demands she made upon his body.

Lachlan frowned. He would be quite happy, he decided, if Aislinn never remembered how she came to be on his land. She seemed pleased with the way things were, and he couldn't remember a time when he had felt quite so… alive. Aislinn's sudden and unexpected appearance in his life had awakened parts of him he hadn't even known existed. There was joy to be found in the simplest of things – a spectacular sunset, a fine tankard of ale, the incredible warmth in a woman's arms – all because of her.

"Come now, Lachlan," Aengus said, sensing the direction of his thoughts. "Ye ken ye will no' have time for the lass today anyway."

"Fine," Lachlan agreed reluctantly. But he didn't have to be happy about it.

* * *

Lachlan clenched his fists tightly at his sides as he saw Malcolm lift Aislinn up onto the mount.

Malcolm's hands lingered just a little too long, and there really was no legitimate reason for him to be that close. The libidinous bastard didn't even like venturing into the village, but as soon as he heard that Simon and Bowen would be taking Aislinn, he had decided to join them. As had Conall and Aengus.

"Does she have to ride with him like that?" Lachlan growled through gritted teeth. Seeing any man – especially Malcolm – touch her like that sent sharp pains through his gut, as if a beast was clawing to get free.

"She can no' ride a mount," Gavin said reasonably beside him. As Gavin was the only one to remain behind at the keep with him, Lachlan decided that he was his most favored kinsman in that moment. "'Tis for her safety. And she seems te have taken a liking te the shameless rogue."

Lachlan grunted. It had more to do with Malcolm wanting her rubbing up against him than anything else, and the bastard knew it. There was no mistaking the smug grin on Malcolm's face.

"She could ride the mare. 'Tis a gentle enough creature for a novice."

"The mare is being shoe'ed today," Gavin answered, a twinkle in his eye. No doubt Lachlan was already suspecting that the shoeing was a last minute request with an ulterior motive.

While Lachlan contemplated several painful ways to kill his brother, Aislinn turned and saw him. She smiled brightly at the sight of him and waved. Then she lifted her fingers to her lips, kissed them, and blew the kiss toward him. Somewhere deep inside his chest, Lachlan's heart clenched.

He watched them until they disappeared from sight, then sighed. It was going to be a very long day without the ability to steal away for a few minutes here and there to see Aislinn. To see her glance up from one of those books she so loved and smile, knowing the smile was for him and him alone. Or to feel her hands kneading upon his shoulders beneath the shade of the old Wych Elm – how she loved to sit beneath that tree in the heat of the day…

Gavin clasped his hand on Lachlan's shoulder as they walked back toward the keep. "I am going te miss the lass," Gavin murmured.

Lachlan stilled. "What did you say?"

Gavin blew out a breath. "Come now, Lachlan. Ye ken she can no' be here when Elyse and her family arrive. 'Twould be too cruel."

With horror, Lachlan suddenly remembered the appointments he had. "Elyse…" Lachlan paled, sinking down onto the low stone wall that surrounded the inner courtyard when his knees went weak.

"Ye did no' tell Aislinn ye were betrothed, did ye, Lachlan?" asked Gavin, his voice soft and only slightly reproachful.

"Nay. In truth, I had forgotten myself. How

does a mon forget his own marriage?"

Gavin nodded somberly. "We figured as much. But then, Aislinn is the type of woman who can make a mon forget many a things, I'm thinking. Even a betrothal."

Lachlan groaned. "Why did ye no' remind me?"

"Because," Gavin said heavily, "for the first time ye seemed truly happy. Even if it was only te last for a few days, none of us was willing te take that away from ye, Lachlan. Ye spent yer whole life taking care of the rest of us, with little or no thought te yerself. We wanted ye te have this time."

Lachlan buried his face in his hands. How had he made such a horrible mess of things in such a short amount of time?

"No one thinks too poorly of ye. 'Tis natural for a mon te lose a wee bit of sense the week afore his wedding." He patted Lachlan on the arm. "But ye ken why Aislinn can no' be here."

Yes, he understood. Because it would kill Aislinn to find out that while he had been seducing her, he had promised himself to another. A woman whose very existence he had forgotten the moment he saw Aislinn.

It felt like a betrayal, more so to Aislinn than to Elyse, though it was Elyse with whom he had an accord. In truth, he made Aislinn no such promise, nor had he ever spoken beyond the moments they shared. Nor had she ever asked, ever hinted that she expected anything more.

"Does she ken?" Lachlan could barely speak.

"Nay. We thought te wait until she was away from Dubhain. Malcolm will be the one te tell her," Gavin said quietly. "She seems te have taken te him. He will explain how it was all set in motion ere she came."

"It will hurt her." He could picture it so clearly in his mind. The flashing sparkle in her eyes would fade, the soft lines in her face would harden, becoming an unreadable mask. The vision speared through him like a lance to the chest.

"No doubt," Gavin agreed solemnly. "But nay so much as if she learned the truth upon Lady Elyse's arrival."

Lachlan understood, too, what Gavin was not saying. That Aislinn would most likely not take the truth quietly. All of that passion simmering just below the surface – the passion she had been gifting him with every day and night – would find a different outlet. It was better that she vent her rage far away from the ears of his future in-laws, away from the people of Dubhain, while surrounded by five braw men who would ensure she would neither cause nor come to harm in the process of doing so. At least now he understood the eagerness of his brethren to accompany her. The woman had enough skills to wreak havoc should she be so inclined.

"Aislinn is both intelligent and strong," Gavin continued. "While she will no' be happy with ye, she will ken the benefits of the agreement and she will endure."

Lachlan didn't want her to *endure*. He wanted her to be happy. No, the hell with that. He wanted her *here*, with *him*. Suddenly everything he would gain from a marriage to Elyse seemed to pale in comparison to the thought of losing Aislinn.

"Lady Elyse is a good woman. Ye may even come te love her, in time."

Gavin meant well, but Lachlan knew better. He would never love Elyse, because he loved Aislinn. He had from the very first moment she had appeared, risking her life to save him, he realized. That was the kind of love he wanted. The kind that struck strong and true and left you feeling dazed afterwards.

Elyse was a good woman, but she would never sass him. She would never spar with him, or lift his kilt and giggle mischievously. She would never wear a man's trews or adorn her womanly parts or tease him with a little silver egg…

"Simon has arranged a meeting in the village with the mon who claims te be Isobeille McKenna's betrothed," Gavin was saying.

Lachlan paled further, feeling ill. "Ye sneaking bastards," he managed to grit out. "Ye knew I would no' allow that."

"Cease thinking of yerself, Lachlan!" Gavin snapped. "Think of Aislinn."

"I *am* thinking of her." He couldn't seem to

think of anything *but* her. "She is no' Isobeille."

"If no', then no harm done. Sir Galen will go on his merry way and continue the search for his betrothed."

"And what of Aislinn? Do ye think te just leave her in the village like an unwanted stray?"

"Malcolm and the others will see that she has all she needs. Simon says he has called in a few favors from a family that has agreed te take her in without asking too many questions. Now," he said, standing up and placing his hand on Lachlan's shoulder, "ye best go get yerself cleaned up before yer bride arrives.

Chapter 10

Aislinn heard the words, but it was taking a while for the reality to sink in.

The handsome older man she had been introduced to earlier as they lunched in the cozy little tavern was Sir Galen Anderson, the betrothed of Isobeille McKenna. Despite her repeated assertions that she was categorically not the missing woman, the Brodies had chosen to go ahead and set up this meeting behind her back anyway. She could not tell if they were relieved or disappointed when Galen agreed that while she did bear a striking physical resemblance, she was not 'his Isobeille'.

That was strike one.

Then, when she asked that they take her back to Dubhain, they told her that she would not be returning. Instead, she was being sent to stay with a family several days' ride away. A family who had generously offered to take her in under the guise of a distant cousin who had been in a terrible accident and had suffered the loss of her memory. She'd been moved around the system often enough as a kid to know when she was being ditched, no matter how pretty a spin they put on it.

That was strike two.

And, when she demanded to know *why* she was being sent away, they told her that Lachlan was betrothed to the daughter of a wealthy landowner. The bride-to-be and her family were arriving at the keep that very day for the impending wedding, which they had been planning for nearly two years and would take place in one week's time.

Strike three.

The death blow.

Game. Over.

Surrounding her in the small room above the tavern that they had secured for her, they watched her closely as if waiting for her to explode. She didn't. She remained calm and still. After sitting in silence for several minutes, Aislinn stood and thanked them for their honesty, then asked them to leave so she might have a few private moments to process all that they had told her.

She wished them a goodnight, making those who would not be escorting her to her new home promise to say goodbye before they rode back to Dubhain the next day. Then she closed the door quietly behind them. Only after several minutes did Aislinn step behind the privacy screen and empty the contents of her stomach into the chamber pot.

"She took that a little too well, dinnae she?" observed Malcolm.

"Aye, that she did," nodded Bowen wearily, rubbing at the spot in his chest where his ribs came together. "Does anyone else feel as though he has been pierced through the heart?" A few murmured agreement.

"I fear she will try te do something ill-advised," said Conall. "Mayhap we should take shifts outside her door."

They all agreed that was a good idea, and devised a watch schedule.

* * *

For the first time in a very long time, Aislinn was terrified. What had begun as a wonderful dream was now turning into a nightmare. She was stuck in a strange dream in a strange land, and she had absolutely no idea what to do. And, real or not, the man she loved – yes, *loved* - the first man she had given her heart to, had sent her away so that she wouldn't be anywhere near when his wife-to-be arrived.

Some part of her – the reality-based, logical part that seemed curiously absent the last week or so - understood. It happened all the time. Not to her, of course – until now she had been way too smart for that sort of thing, but she'd seen it happen enough to others to know.

She'd been a novelty. Something different, something fun for him to play with. But not for keeps. She could not fool herself into thinking she was a laird's wife. She was his personal whore, a final fling. And she, dumb shit that she was, had allowed herself to fall in love. It was beyond stupid.

He hadn't even had the balls to tell her himself. No, the bastard had smiled and waved as he had his brothers cart her away in the hopes that Sir Galen would claim her, with the contingency plan of shipping her off to the sticks if that little plan fell through. The bottom line: Aislinn had worn out her welcome.

At least the brothers had been honest with her, explaining things as gently as possible. Not an easy thing to do when you're ripping someone's heart out. And before they broke the bad news, they had taken her shopping, buying her proper dresses and baubles and showing her around, pointing out things of interest and telling her funny stories. They had tried to soften the blow.

She could almost feel bad for them. *Almost*. But then she thought of the pity she'd seen in their eyes and her fear turned to anger. She was not a woman to be pitied. She'd had enough of that over her life. Pity didn't fill your belly or heal your bruises.

Unbidden, there was no stopping the echoing whispers inside her head.

"Poor thing, her whole family's gone."

"Look at the tiny child. Have you ever seen so many bruises?"

"I'm sorry, Aislinn. You leave me no choice. If you insist on misbehaving..."

"They're all dead, the whole unit. How's she going to live with that if she pulls through?"

"'Tis for the best, lass."

It was the last one, the most recent, that resounded the loudest. Aislinn covered her ears as if she could stop the voices. Forcing herself to focus, she locked them all away one by one.

"It is a smart match. 'Tis for the best, lass."

They'd taken great pains to explain to her how Dubhain and its people would benefit from the marriage, how it would elevate the Brodie clan in terms of respect and power. How Lachlan had worked on the union for the past two years. His bride had land, a dowry. Came from a good and influential family. It *was* a smart marriage, at least from a business perspective.

And Lachlan *did* care for his people; that was apparent in everything he did. It gave her some small comfort to think that maybe, way deep down, he would miss her a little bit, too. That he was the type of man who would sacrifice his own wants and needs for those he cared about, those to whom he felt a responsibility. Lachlan had been their laird, their overseer, their protector for twenty years, and she'd known him for what – a week? It didn't take a rocket scientist to figure out which side the scales tipped to there.

Sucked ass for her, though.

"She has been raised to be a laird's wife. 'Tis for the best, lass."

Just when she was starting to feel a little less murderous, that lovely nugget had to re-surface.

Lachlan was a man in a position of power. He deserved a proper bride, one who would dress and act the part because she had been born to it. One who could play the perfect hostess. One who would not embarrass him by something she said or did every time she turned around.

Aislinn could almost picture his bride. She'd be quiet, demure. She'd wear beautiful gowns without complaint and keep her eyes downcast, speaking only when spoken to. Her skin would be soft and pale, her hands delicate and uncalloused. She would hold a needle and thread in her hand, not blades and guns, and she would expect her husband to see to her every need.

Quite simply, she was everything Aislinn was not. Could never be.

"'Tis a quiet place where yer mind may yet heal. 'Tis for the best, lass."

That hurt almost as much as everything else. The fact that these men of whom she'd become so fond so quickly still thought there was something wrong with her. That all this time, they had merely been humoring her until they could carry out their plans to get rid of her.

It was more than she could take.

She didn't want to be in this dream anymore.

It was time to wake up.

* * *

Lachlan sank heavily into his bed, the same bed in which he had awoken so wonderfully this morning with Aislinn warm and solid against him. With little more than a simple caress along her inner thigh, an unspoken request, she had welcomed him willingly, filling his heart even as he filled her body. To think that it was the last time he would know such joy…

To have a day begin with such promise and end with such despair was cruel, he decided.

He lifted the eiderdown pillow and inhaled, taking what little remained of Aislinn into him. No, that wasn't really true. Aislinn was already there. In only a few days, she had managed to burrow deep inside him, soaked into his heart and his soul, and no matter what he was forced to do now and in the coming days, she would always be there.

Elyse and her family had arrived as expected. She was every bit as lovely as she had been the last time Lachlan had seen her, but it was a cold kind of beauty; one that was fashioned by a skillful hand and funded by her affluent father's coin. As lovely as she was, she held none of Aislinn's fire and passion.

Elyse was a vain woman, Lachlan realized. Even travelling, she wore an exquisite gown crafted from the finest fabrics. Her neck and wrists had been adorned with gems and finely-worked precious metals.

"*I wonder how many hungry mouths she could feed if she swallowed some of that vanity and sold one of those necklaces.*" Aislinn's words came to mind unbidden, the ones she spoke to Lachlan privately when she had seen a similarly dressed laird's wife.

The laird, whose land bordered Dubhain on the east, had come to inform Lachlan that his men had managed to capture several of the McCraes who had thought to take refuge in his land. The man himself was a decent enough sort, had been a friend and ally of the Brodies for many years, but his wife was a nasty piece of work. Aislinn's words came after Lachlan told her that several of the man's bastards now apprenticed at Dubhain, turned out by the laird's wife who was as jealous as they came.

Elyse was not just vain, but spoiled as well. After only a few moments of requisite pleasantries, Elyse had informed them all that she would be retiring, exhausted by the long journey. Even though she had done little more than lounge in the back of the comfortable carriage, he thought. Then she proceeded to provide him with a very long list of the things she would be requiring. He'd had to dispatch no less than half a dozen servants to see to her needs, let alone the rest of her entourage.

Aislinn never made such demands. The woman

washed her own clothing in the bath water; made her own fire in the hearth; emptied her own chamber pot. She was averse to asking for anything, really, preferring to see to her own needs. When Lachlan spoke with her about it, she'd said, "After spending a majority of my life serving others, I'll be damned if I'll make anyone serve me." When he responded that that was their job, she'd said, "Believe me, they are already earning every dime." He wasn't sure what a dime was, but she'd made her point.

It wasn't just herself she took care of, either. Aislinn was forever looking after the lads like a right mother hen, spending time with them, making sure they had enough to eat and clothes to wear. She told them outrageous stories of faraway lands and mind-boggling gadgets; in return, they were teaching her to speak his native Gaelic.

They had taken to her, too. He wondered what they would think when they realized she wasn't coming back; Lachlan couldn't imagine Elyse filling that hole. Hell. He couldn't even imagine Elyse with their own children. But Aislinn… Aislinn he had no trouble picturing growing round with his young, or holding them in her arms, suckling them, protecting them with her very life like a fierce mama bear…

His bedchamber suddenly felt very cold and empty, though everything was in perfect order. A fire blazed in the hearth, but he didn't feel its heat.

A small repast sat, untouched, on the scarred table, along with a tankard of ale.

Lachlan had no appetite, but he took the ale. As he tipped the tankard and let it fill his belly, he wondered if this is how the rest of his life was going to be. Pretty to look at from the outside, but bereft of warmth.

As he walked to the window to gaze out upon the now-silent courtyard below, Lachlan's eyes came to rest upon the small black shape tucked in the far corner of the room. He immediately recognized it as Aislinn's pack, for there was nothing else like it. It seemed strange that it should be here when she was not.

Of course she wouldn't have taken it with her, he thought bitterly. She had trusted them. She had thought she'd be returning.

Feeling as though his body had been hollowed out and refilled with stone, Lachlan found himself crossing the room and picking it up. Material things meant so very little to Aislinn, but she would want this. This small satchel held all of her most prized possessions. He would talk to Simon upon his return, ask that the pack be sent to Aislinn, wherever that was. Gavin had refused to tell him, and that was probably a good thing. If he knew, no doubt he would already be halfway there, needing to see her just one more time.

And what would he tell her? *I'm sorry?*

He grunted into the silence. Sorry didn't begin

to cover it. But he was a laird, goddamnit. He needed to put the welfare of his people above his own selfish desires. This arrangement had been two years in the making, crafted to achieve maximum benefit for those who lived and worked in Dubhain. Marrying Elyse would extend their boundaries, bloat their coffers, and ensure that their trenchers remained full for many years to come.

But they weren't so bad off, were they? His keep might not be the wealthiest, but his people did not go hungry, nor were the sick and infirmed neglected. And they were a happy lot by nature, the strength of their bonds far more than that forged on coin or fear. No, Dubhain had grown right along with Lachlan; it was a strong, healthy community. Good people, with good hearts. He owed them the best he could give them, didn't he?

He stared at the pack for a long time before he finally worked up the courage to open it. Aislinn had been very protective of it. The few times he'd tried to peek inside she'd snatched it out of his hands, her cheeks pink, saying that what was inside was "personal".

If she was here, he would have continued to respect her wish for privacy. But Aislinn was gone, and he could not resist the urge to have one last chance at knowing the woman who had captured his heart.

With trembling hands, Lachlan extracted the items one by one and arranged them on the table.

Only once the pack was empty and everything was laid out before him would he allow himself to study each item with the reverence it deserved.

There was a small device that fit easily in his hand, crafted of some unfamiliar material. He thought at first it might be similar to the silver orb she had shared with him, but this one was a soft pink color with unusual symbols and writing on the side and did not appear to vibrate. While examining it, he discovered one end came off. Lifting it to his nose, he recognized the soft, fresh scent he associated with the particularly tender areas along the sides of her breasts. Determining that it was some sort of fragrance, he let the familiar aroma fill his lungs and set it aside. Mayhap he would keep that one.

Next, he looked at a long stick with some kind of short, stiff bristles arising from one end. He had actually seen her use this once when she thought he was still sleeping. She had squeezed some pasty white substance on the bristles and then moved it around in her mouth for a while before rinsing. When she returned to bed, her mouth had the delicious taste of peppermint. Mayhap he would hold on to that one, as well.

His focus turned to a leather pouch. When unfolded, it revealed several small pockets, each of which held one of the shiny weapons he'd seen her use that first day. Extracting one, he found it extremely sharp, sucking his thumb where he had inadvertently punctured it with one especially honed tip. He had never seen anything like them, but Aislinn had wielded them expertly that day. Each was immaculately cleaned and sharp. Lachlan had respect for someone who took such care of their weapons. She should have them with her; if he could not take care of her, he would at least do everything he could to ensure she could take care of herself.

He examined and quickly discarded what appeared to be a roll of rectangular papers, greenish in color and marked with unfamiliar pictures and writing. If he had to guess, he would think it was some form of currency, but he had little interest in that. He set those aside, along with a small hairbrush.

He saved the most interesting-looking items for last. One was a glass bottle half-filled with an amber liquid. After managing to remove the top (he had to twist, not pull, the odd cork), Lachlan lifted the bottle to his lips and smiled as he recognized the aroma of fine whiskey. Perhaps he should have felt some shock at finding such a strong spirit amongst a female's things, but this was Aislinn, after all. Without apology, he lifted the bottle to his lips and drank in both toast and tribute, welcoming the smooth, slow burn.

The last item appeared to be a book, but it was unlike any tome he had ever seen. Several inches thick, hardly bigger than his hand, the tops and bottoms appeared to be made of a thin parchment. Lachlan sucked a breath through his teeth when he took a closer look at the faded picture on the well-worn cover. It appeared to be that of a braw Highlander trapping a comely maiden in his arms, his intent clear by the hungry expression on the warrior's face.

Lachlan knew that look. It was the same one he had whenever he saw Aislinn.

He opened the cover gently, for the book appeared as if it was ready to fall apart in his hands. He turned through the first couple of pages quickly – he could make neither heads nor tails of them – until he came to the beginning of the story. Then Lachlan Brodie began to read.

Even as well-versed in English as he was, there was much that Lachlan didn't understand. It took him most of the night, but he did read it all. By the time he was finished, the dawn was nigh and the bottle of whiskey had long since been emptied.

And Lachlan Brodie, Laird of Dubhain, knew what he had to do.

Chapter 11

"Any sign of her?" Malcolm asked as he came to relieve Bowen in front of Aislinn's door. The sun had risen hours earlier. They had all washed and eaten; the horses were packed and ready to go.

"Nay," Bowen said, shaking his head. "But Simon said he heard her crying late inte the night."

Malcolm nodded, but could not ease the sense of dread that had begun the moment she had closed the door on them the night before and had been increasing ever since. He knocked on the door. "Aislinn." He hesitated, awaiting a response and receiving none. "Aislinn, dearling, I have brought ye something te break yer fast."

Silence.

"Come now, Aislinn. Conall, Bowen and I must be gettin' back and we wish te keep our promise te ye."

Several of the others joined him in the hallway, looking every bit as concerned as he felt. Without further preamble, Malcolm reached down and grasped the latch with a final warning, ready to break the door down if necessary. There was no need. It opened easily with the slightest pressure.

The bed was made, even neater than it had been on their initial arrival. The fire had been snuffed, the blackened embers cold to the touch. On the bed was the gown Aislinn had been wearing, along with the several they had purchased for her the day before. On the scarred table was the small purse of coins they had given her, as well as a note, hand-scratched with a charred piece of wood from the hearth.

"Thanks, but no thanks. Best wishes to the laird and his betrothed. –A."

* * *

Among other things, Aislinn had been blessed with an excellent sense of direction. It was a skill perhaps not among the most coveted, but for a woman who found herself in unfamiliar lands more often than not, it was greatly appreciated.

After much thought, Aislinn decided the best place to end her dream was where it had all begun. Travelling on foot and only by the light of the moon made her progress slow, but that was alright. It wasn't really like she had anywhere else to be.

It had been child's play for a woman with her training to scale the outside walls of the tavern silently and without being seen; even more so to steal clothes that would disguise her appearance.

Aislinn could be a ghost when she wanted to. Keeping to the shadows, wishing she'd had the foresight to bring her pack with her yesterday, Aislinn slipped out of the village, and away from the well-meaning but misguided Brodies, unnoticed.

For a brief amount of time, Aislinn considered remaining in her dream state, just changing the scenery a little. She had nothing to go back to, really. Not that she had anything here, either, but it almost seemed as if it would be easier to carve out a life for herself here than back in her own reality. There were plenty of places a well-seasoned veteran like her could all but disappear. She'd be a burden to no one, answer to no one. Of course, she'd be alone, too, but she was used to that.

As desirable as that seemed, Aislinn knew in her heart she couldn't stay. No matter how far she travelled, she would always have to fight the urge to return to Dubhain. To see Lachlan, if only from afar.

Except it wouldn't be just Lachlan that she saw. She would see his wife and his children, too.

And that, she knew, would kill her.

It took three nights, but she finally arrived back at the clearing where she had first awoken in her dream. It would end here, just as it had begun.

She thought back to when she had seen Lachlan for the first time. How beautiful and fierce he had been as he fought off six men at once. If she was truly honest with herself, she'd have to admit she'd probably fallen in love with him right then and there. So proud and handsome…

She walked around, filling herself with the sights and scents and feel of this surreal place before dropping down beneath the same tree where she'd awoken. It had been a little more than a week ago that she had opened her eyes in this wondrous land, but it felt more like a lifetime. Wishing she had her Jack instead – she and Jack were always tight when things went south - Aislinn pulled out the bottle of whiskey she'd managed to slip away with. Funny; she hadn't had the desire for a drink since she got here, but then, she'd had plenty of other things on her mind, hadn't she?

The first swallow went down a little harder than she was used to, but it was a welcome and familiar-enough burn that she relished all the way down her throat, heat blossoming in her empty stomach as it landed there. She had not bothered to eat on her final journey. It was a dream, after all, and given the way she felt when she'd first arrived, the less she had on her stomach when she re-awoke back at home, the better.

The same logic did not apply to alcohol, however. She took another drink, and another, until there was no more. It was not nearly enough.

Aislinn lay there for a long time, the feel of the fallowed grass strangely comforting beneath her. Despite her exhaustion and the numbing effects of the potent spirits, sleep remained elusive. She replayed scenes from the last week over and over in her mind. She would keep the happy memories. Even with everything that happened, Dubhain and the Brodies had given her more good memories than the rest of her life combined. And how pathetic was that?

She saw the motion in the periphery of her vision, the slight swish of the grass the only sound. She watched with mild interest as the snake neared.

It was ironic in a cruel and poetic way. This clearing had been her Eden of sorts. It was only fitting that her time here end with the appearance of a serpent. It was classic Old Testament, and Aislinn had always been more comfortable with the whole "eye for an eye" thing than the "turn the other cheek" concept – at least, one was clearly more prevalent in her life than the other.

She sent up a prayer of both thanks and apology; the thanks for the answered prayer she'd uttered at midnight Mass, the apology for her hubris in asking in the first place.

"Well, come on then," she prodded, only mildly slurring the words. "Take me home." Wherever that might be.

Aislinn extended her arm. The adder wasted no time in striking, not once, but three times. The bites were beyond painful, but Aislinn refused to make a sound. She'd known worse pain, and physical pain was nothing when your heart had been shattered.

It didn't take long for the venom to make itself

known. The adder's strikes had been sure and true. Excruciating pain at each bite site became a caustic burning in her veins. She could feel the poison making its way through her body. And with each beat of her heart, it hurt a little less, until she felt practically nothing at all. Minutes later, she thought she might have felt the first rays of the dawn on her face even as Lachlan's voice calling her name echoed in her brain, a bittersweet goodbye.

* * *

Lachlan Brodie roared out to the heavens as he galloped back toward his keep at breakneck speed, the tiny limp figure in his arms. Thank God he had posted watchers all around the clearing. Thank God that after three days of fruitless searching, Conall had reasoned that she might return to where it had all begun.

Long before he reached the gates a crowd had rushed out to meet him.

"Jesu!" Malcolm cursed as he saw the woman in Lachlan's arms. Her face was deathly white, streaked with the dark blue and purple lines of her poisoned veins below the surface. Her limbs hung limply, one arm covered in blood, swollen beyond recognition from the multiple piercings of deadly fangs.

Chapter 12

"I found her near the clearing," Lachlan said quietly, brushing the hair back from her face with trembling fingers. "'Twas an adder that bit her. I saw it. Even as I dropped to my knees beside her, it reared up in the grass and *looked* at me afore slithering away."

It was the first time he had spoken in days. Since he'd found her and brought her back to the keep, Lachlan had not left her side, speaking only to Aislinn as she remained beyond their reach. Malcolm was not about to stop him now.

"It nearly killed me te cut her," Lachlan said, his eyes growing dark as he remembered crying out as the blade sliced her skin so he could draw out the poison.

"Ye saved her life."

No, thought Lachlan, he had failed miserably at protecting the one thing that meant more to him than anything else in the world. According to the physician, it had been the copious amounts of alcohol that had kept her alive long enough for Lachlan to find her. Her system had been so retarded by it the poison hadn't had a chance to take full effect.

Though she had yet to open her eyes, her heart was beating, albeit weakly and erratically. Her breaths were shallow and filled with an ominous rattle that he refused to acknowledge. Her skin had been so hot to the touch that Lachlan had taken it upon himself to bathe her with cool water frequently; then she would shake uncontrollably and he would wrap her in the softest, warmest blankets he could find and crawl into bed with her in the hopes that the heat from his body would soak into her. He would patiently wet her lips and squeeze droplets of water into her mouth, experiencing a small victory each time she swallowed reflexively.

It was heartbreaking. Despite all of their efforts, every few hours she would gasp and seize, and it took him and several of his brothers to hold her in place so she would not further injure herself.

She had been still for the last several hours, her body serene.

Before leaving, the healer had told them this night Aislinn would decide whether to stay or go.

It would cost Dubhain dearly to nullify the marriage contract that had been drawn between the clans, but he had the full and unwavering support of his brothers. Sir William, Elyse's father, was understandably upset, but perhaps not as much as he might have been. Lachlan knew he had made the right decision when Elyse simply bowed her head and accepted the change in plans with grace and decorum.

Aislinn would have pitched a bloody fit, and that's what Lachlan wanted: a woman who loved him enough to fight for him.

Just as he would fight for her.

Lachlan took Aislinn's tiny hands in his and kneeled beside the bed. Then he bowed his head and began to pray with all of his heart.

* * *

Aislinn awoke slowly, cocooned in the most wonderful warmth. Feeling stiff, as if she'd lain in the same position for too long, she attempted to turn. Strong male arms tightened around her. She forced her eyes open and found her face snuggled into a familiar neck. She inhaled deeply, drawing Lachlan's scent into her as if starved for it.

Unable to think of anything else, she focused all of her attention on the wonderful feel of his naked body flush against hers, the searing heat from his skin as it soaked into hers. At the strong, steady beat of his heart against her belly. She nuzzled him, her tongue peeking out for just a slight taste.

Lachlan stiffened. "Aislinn?" He pulled back enough to look into her face, his eyes wild with hope. "Aislinn? Ah, thank God, ye came back te me, lass." His lips were hard yet oddly tender against hers when she felt the first hot tears on her cheek. Lachlan was crying?

That quickly, the images started coming back to her. Blowing Lachlan a kiss as she waved goodbye. Malcolm and the others explaining how she had to leave because Lachlan was to wed another. How she had made her way back to the clearing, wanting to go home.

But she wasn't home.

"Lachlan." Her throat protested as she forced the name out, little more than a hoarse bark.

"Shhhh, doona try te talk yet, loving." Suddenly there was a cup at her lips and he was urging her to drink. Desperate with thirst, she wrapped both of her hands around his and pulled the cup toward her. "Easy, loving, easy," he crooned in her ear as he controlled the cup, only letting a few drops in at a time.

"More," she rasped when the cup was empty.

"In a wee bit. Yer belly has been empty far too long."

Moments later she was glad he had kept her from guzzling the whole thing as her stomach cramped uncomfortably.

"Why am I here?" she asked, a brief look around telling her she was in Lachlan's private chamber.

"Ye have been ill," he said, his face turning somber. "Verra ill. I have been caring for ye."

"Doesn't your *wife* mind?"

The look of pain Lachlan gave her was like a

full-bodied tackle to her already-tortured soul. Feeling even more sick to her stomach, Aislinn pushed at his chest, only to discover she was a weak as a newborn kitten. Lachlan easily took both of her hands in his much larger one and leaned down to place gentle kisses along her jaw. "Easy, loving. I have ye. Everything is going te be all right."

Aislinn didn't think twice. Summoning every bit of the meager strength she had, she used it for the sudden lift of her knee and the satisfying connection with a certain part of his anatomy.

"Och! What did ye do that for?" he wheezed, turning his hips to prevent her from taking another shot at his manly parts.

Anger, it seemed, went a long way in fueling enough energy for a proper response.

"For being engaged to someone else while you were fucking me for fun. For not telling me yourself. For having your brothers tell me as they were carting me off to some funny farm. *For making me fall in love with you, you stupid bastard.*"

Instead of being angry, he grinned, pinning her arms and legs to keep her from doing further damage as he rose above her. "Ye love me?"

A growl of frustration rumbled up through her chest. Of course that would be the only thing that managed to penetrate that thick, Celtic man-skull of his.

"No," she hissed. "I give my body to every man

a day or so after I meet him."

His smile was gone instantly, replaced by a look of fierce possession. "Ye are mine," he growled. "No other mon will ken the pleasure of yer flesh. *Ever*."

Fire raged in her hazel eyes; if looks could kill, he would have been reduced to fine ash. "You gave up the right to make that decision when you sent me away."

"I did no' send ye away. I thought they were taking ye inte town for the day."

Aislinn snorted. "Yeah, right."

His face hardened, and his voice grew softer, as it always did when he meant business. "Are ye calling me a liar, Aislinn McKenna?"

"Yeah, well if the big, fat shoe fits, you can shove it right up your arrogant, man-whoring *arse*."

His cock grew hard and long against her hip. No one lit a fire inside of him like this woman – this impossible, passionate, beautiful woman. She would always demand his complete and utter devotion, and would never allow him to falter, never accept anything less.

"I never lied te ye, Aislinn. I swear te ye I did no' ken what they had planned."

"But you knew you were getting married, didn't you? Maybe you never came right out and said you were available, but I kind of assumed that, given that you had me in your bed every night. That's called a sin of omission, buddy, and it's every bit as bad as lying."

"I… forgot." It sounded pathetic, even to his own ears.

"You *forgot*?!? Are you fucking kidding me?"

"Ye make me crazy, lass," he exploded, his voice rising right along with his heart rate, the pounding in his ears, and the blood pulsing painfully in his swollen cock. "Ye came inte my life and aye, I simply forgot everything else. *Because nothing else mattered anymore besides ye.*"

That gave her a moment's pause, but she was too far gone in her womanly indignation to stop now. "Yeah? And what of your *wife*? How does she feel about that, *Laird Brodie*?" She spat the title and name as if it was a vile curse.

A heavy sigh. "Ye are the only woman who will be my wife, Aislinn."

That shut her up. For all of about three seconds. "What about *Elyse*?"

"On her way back to her family's lands."

"You're not getting married?"

He leaned down and nipped her bottom lip with his teeth in scolding. It should not have turned her on as much as it did; she was mad at him, goddammit.

"Are ye not listening, lass? O' course I am getting married. But only te ye."

Her mind screamed "arrogant bastard" while her heart simply melted into a puddle deep in her chest. She sniffed and lifted her chin defiantly.

"Maybe I don't *want* to marry you."

"O' course ye do. *Ye love me*." Lachlan grinned like a fool as he leaned down and captured her mouth in a womb-clenching kiss.

* * *

Aislinn didn't make it easy for him. His brothers found great glee in watching the laird of Dubhain grovel and woo his bride. They were quite free with their suggestions on how to further his torment, many of which Aislinn took to heart.

They were not completely off the hook, either. She still resented the fact that they had conspired behind Lachlan's back to ship her off. She was, they discovered soon enough, every bit as sneaky and cunning as any of them.

After nearly a month of waking up feeling like she had the flu, however, Aislinn decided that she had punished Lachlan enough.

It was as she lay next to him in bed, feeling boneless and sated from their particularly vigorous bout of make-up sex – the first she had allowed him to share her bed since awakening two months earlier - that she first broached the subject.

"Why did you agree to marry Elyse if you didn't love her?"

* * *

Lachlan tensed beneath her petting hand. Aislinn had just come back into his bed. He had no wish to say or do anything that might change that, so he pretended to be asleep.

His clever sprite wasn't fooled for a minute. She took several of his chest hairs between her thumb and forefinger and tugged, freeing them from his skin. "Malcolm said it was because you needed to breed some heirs," she prodded.

Clearly he was going to have to work harder at wearing her out if she had the energy to do that, he decided.

"Malcolm does no' ken when te keep his big mouth shut," he grumbled without opening his eyes. His big hand closed over hers in case she planned to pluck a few more hairs from his chest.

Aislinn climbed up on top of him, folding her hands beneath her chin and looking into his eyes. "Is it true?"

She was not going to let this go, he realized. She would not allow him to glide easily along. His woman would always be there, holding him accountable for his actions. He had been a good laird before, but she was making him a fine man. And he loved her for it.

"Aye, 'tis," he admitted with a heavy sigh.

"There are lots of little boys running around the keep with auburn hair and green eyes. Are any of them yours?"

"Nay."

"How come?"

Lachlan slipped his arms behind his head so he could look down at her with luminous green eyes. There was no anger in her tone, nor in her expression, just genuine bemusement. "Are ye asking me why I did no' see fit te sire a bastard?"

"Yes. I mean, you're obviously very skilled in that area," – he smirked smugly at this – "so I know you weren't keeping Mr. Happy in your pants all these years."

He arched a brow, wondering if he would ever *not* be surprised by what came out of her mouth. He sincerely hoped not.

"Nay, I was no' celibate," he agreed. "But I had no wish te breed a child out of wedlock, either. 'Tis different for a laird, ye ken. 'Tis my heirs that will inherit Dubhain, and I did no' think it fair my firstborn be denied that right simply because I did no' fancy his mother enough te wed her."

She considered this, petting him softly once again with her fingertips. It was one of the things he had missed most during their time apart. He wondered if she even realized she was doing it.

"So... a son born to you out of wedlock couldn't inherit Dubhain?"

"Nay. He would be an important member of the clan, but an illegitimate son could hold no title according te our laws."

"Hmmm. Well, I guess that settles it, then."

He looked at her suspiciously. "Settles what?"

The soft petting became a firm (and somewhat painful) poking. "If my calculations are correct, you have about five months to plan our wedding and get us hitched."

It took a while for her words to sink in. When they finally did, his eyes opened wide. "Ye are with child?"

She nodded. In the next moment she was on her back, Lachlan rubbing his hands over her abdomen. "My child rests here?"

"Yep."

He leaned down and kissed her belly with nothing less than reverence. When he looked up at her, his green eyes were shiny.

* * *

Aislinn looked down at him. Her beautiful, fierce laird. The look on his face threatened to steal all of her breath away. Eyes glistening with awe and so much love she felt it, like a warm blanket wrapping around her, melting the last bit of ice around her heart. In that moment, she knew that this man would do anything for her.

Then the first tear fell, hot and wet, on her skin. Followed by another. Lachlan lowered his head and pressed his cheek against her belly. His powerful arms slipped around her and held her tight, as if he was afraid she might slip away if he didn't.

"Lachlan?" she asked, stroking the waves of his

auburn locks.

"I almost lost ye," he whispered against her skin, his barely audible voice thick.

"But you didn't," she answered softly.

"I was a fool, Aislinn."

"No argument there," she agreed, but there was no bite to her tone.

Lachlan lifted his head enough to press kisses against the expanse of now-moist skin from hip to hip. "I." *Kiss.* "Will never." *Kiss.* "Let". *Kiss.* "Ye out." *Kiss.* "Of my sight." *Kiss.* "Again."

The familiar heat began to build in her core with each one, those full, masculine lips nothing short of magical. "Oh?" she hummed, closing her eyes, allowing her other senses to rise to the occasion. "Don't I have anything to say about that?"

He nipped at her hip. "Nay. Ye are mine."

There was something incredibly hot about a possessive, aroused Highlander, she decided. No wonder it was such a popular romance genre. Aislinn bent one leg at the knee to stroke the proof of his interest with her calf. Doing so also had the added benefit of opening her up to him.

He cast his eyes up to hers and grinned wickedly. "Something ye be wantin', lass?"

Her core clenched. His brogue always thickened when he was really aroused, just as his clear green eyes darkened to fine emeralds.

"No," she lied.

His eyes blazed. "Liar," he breathed, lowering

his head to nuzzle her. She *might* have whimpered. Just a little.

"Ask, loving. All ye have te do is ask."

The smug bastard was torturing her. He knew exactly what she wanted. Knew that with every light rub of his slightly-whiskered jaw against the inside of her thighs he was driving her crazy. She gripped his hair, hard, and tried to angle her hips to position herself exactly where she needed to be.

He laughed, staying so close but just out of reach. The deep rumble, combined with the hot puffs of air over her most sensitive bundle of nerves nearly sent her over the edge. It was against her nature to ask for anything, so the breathy, desperate plea that left her lips was unexpected.

"Please," she begged.

Surprise lit his eyes. Surprise and something else. Something inherently carnal. "That'll do, lass."

He kissed her tenderly, slowly. Drew out her passion with long, languorous licks and gentle sucks and pulls until she thought she just might die from the exquisite torture.

"Lachlan," she wheezed. Fully focused on his task, he did not hear her at first. "Lachlan," she said again, adding a substantial tug on his locks to gain his attention. He looked up at her, his eyes heavy and dazed with desire. If her heart hadn't already melted, it would have in that moment.

"I want you inside me."

His eyes blazed. With one last kiss he moved

up her body, settling in the cradle of her thighs. Her arms and legs wrapped around him as she finally spoke the words that had never once passed her lips: "I love you."

His mouth sealed over hers as he slid deep, and Aislinn knew that her wish had finally been granted.

Epilogue

Six Months Later

"He is perfect," Lachlan said softly, cradling his son in his arms. Small downy wisps of auburn, a bit darker than Lachlan's, covered the boy's head; his eyes, already fading from the newborn blue, were a unique combination of mother and father – a clear, luminous green ringed by a beautiful amber around the edges. It had been a long labor – the boy had the brawn of a true Brodie, but his wee wife was a strong, fit woman. Not for the first time, he was thankful for that. "I want at least a dozen more."

Aislinn, too exhausted to lift her head, laughed into the pillow.

"Fine, braw lads, o' course," he continued. "But I was thinking that Dubhain could use a few more bonnie lasses about as weel."

"I'll see what I can do about that," she mumbled sleepily, making him chuckle. He could not imagine a man happier than he was at that very moment.

"I think ye were right after all, Aislinn, my love."

"Of course I was," she agreed without hesitation. "About what?"

"It does feel like a dream."

She was surprised by his words. Neither of them had spoken of dreams or her sudden appearance since he'd found her in the clearing and brought her back to Dubhain. They were no closer to explaining how she came to be there, but it no longer mattered. And, as Aislinn adjusted to her new life as if she had been born to it, no one really even thought of it anymore.

But sometimes, in the middle of the night, Aislinn would snuggle against her big, warm husband and remember her last night in the city. Of bowing her head at midnight Mass and offering that one desperate prayer: to know true love.

Aislinn believed, with all of her heart, that her prayer had been answered. It didn't matter why or how.

Offering up a silent prayer of thanks, she leaned against her husband and kissed her son's feathery soft head. She gave Lachlan a smile, the kind she reserved only for him. "If it is, then I never want to wake up."

He smiled right back at her, encompassing her and their son in his large, powerful arms, and she knew she was there to stay. Her laird would make sure of it.

Glossary

afore	before
albeit	although
amnae	am not
aye	yes
behoove	to be necessary or proper for
cannae	can not
coffer	treasury, funds
dinnae	did not
doesna	does not
doona	do not
garderobe	a medieval bathroom
inte	Into
isnae	is not
ken	know, understand, comprehend, perceive
laird	lord, overseer
mayhap	maybe, perhaps
mon	man
sennight	week
te	to
tome	book
trencher	plate
trews	close-fitting trousers
untoward	improper
verra	very
wee	small, little, tiny
wouldnae	would not
ye	you

Thanks for reading Aislinn's story

Have you read Part I? Remember Newton's Third Law: For every action, there is an equal and opposite reaction. If Aislinn went back, then someone else had to go forward.

If you want to see what happens when a 15th century Scottish peasant girl suddenly finds herself dropped into the heart of modern-day NYC, check out Isobeille's story in **Maiden in Manhattan** (originally released under the title "Lost in Time I").

If you liked this book, then please consider posting a review online! It's really easy, only takes a few minutes, and makes a huge difference to independent authors who don't have the mega-budgets of the big-time publishers behind them.

Log on to your favorite online retailer (or Goodreads) and just tell others what you thought, even if it's just a line or two. That's it! A good review is one of the nicest things you can do for any author.

As always, I welcome feedback. Email me at abbiezandersromance@gmail.com. Or sign up for my mailing list on my website at https://abbiezandersromance.com for up to date info and advance notices on new releases, Like my FB page (AbbieZandersRomance), and/or follow me on Twitter (@AbbieZanders).

Thanks again, and may all of your ever-afters be happy ones!

❤ *Abbie*

Also by Abbie Zanders

Contemporary Romance – Callaghan Brothers

Plan your visit to Pine Ridge, Pennsylvania and fall in love with the Callaghans

- Dangerous Secrets
- First and Only
- House Calls
- Seeking Vengeance
- Guardian Angel
- Beyond Affection
- Having Faith
- Bottom Line
- Forever Mine
- Two of a Kind
- Not Quite Broken

Contemporary Romance – Connelly Cousins

Drive across the river to Birch Falls and spend some time with the Connelly Cousins

- Celina
- Jamie
- Johnny
- Michael

Contemporary Romance – Covendale Series

If you like humor and snark in your romance, add a stop in Covendale

- 📖 Five Minute Man
- 📖 All Night Woman
- 📖 Seizing Mack

Contemporary Romance – Sanctuary

More small town romance with former military heroes you can't help but love

- 📖 Protecting Sam
- 📖 Best Laid Plans
- 📖 Shadow of Doubt

More Contemporary Romance

- 📖 The Realist
- 📖 Celestial Desire
- 📖 Letting Go
- 📖 SEAL Out of Water (Silver SEALs)

Cerasino Family Novellas

Short, sweet romance to put a smile on your face

- Just For Me
- Just For Him

Time Travel Romance

Travel between present day NYC and 15th century Scotland in these stand-alone but related titles

- Maiden in Manhattan
- Raising Hell in the Highlands

Paranormal Romance – Mythic Series

Welcome to Mythic, an idyllic communities all kinds of Extraordinaries call home.

- Faerie Godmother
- Fallen Angel
- The Oracle at Mythic
- Wolf Out of Water

More Paranormal Romance

- Vampire, Unaware
- Black Wolfe's Mate (written as Avelyn McCrae)
- Going Nowhere
- The Jewel
- Close Encounters of the Sexy Kind
- Rock Hard
- Immortal Dreams
- Rehabbing the Beast (written as Avelyn McCrae)
- More Than Mortal

Howls Romance

Classic romance with a furry twist

- Falling for the Werewolf
- A Very Beary Christmas

Historical/Medieval Romance

- A Warrior's Heart (written as Avelyn McCrae)

About the Author

Abbie Zanders loves to read and write romance in all forms; she is quite obsessive, really. Her ultimate fantasy is to spend all of her free time doing both, preferably in a secluded mountain cabin overlooking a pristine lake, though a private beach on a lush tropical island works, too. Sharing her work with others of similar mind is a dream come true. She promises her readers two things: no cliffhangers, and there will always be a happy ending. Beyond that, you never know…

Printed in Great Britain
by Amazon